Griffith

THE ENGLISH DRAGON BOOK 5

KATHI S. BARTON

World Castle Publishing, LLC
Pensacola, Florida
Copyright © Kathi S. Barton 2018
Paperback ISBN: 9781629899794
eBook ISBN: 9781629899800
First Edition World Castle Publishing, LLC, August 20, 2018
http://www.worldcastlepublishing.com

Licensing Notes
Cover: Karen Fuller
Editor: Maxine Bringenberg

Chapter 1

Kip moved along the walls and decided he didn't care for the smell or this place in any way. Not now, at least. After it was abandoned, it had become a place to flop for all manner of things. It was dirty, filled with scents that made even his dragon sick. Well, he was going to take care of this place, once and for all. As soon as he was able to shift so he could burn the place to the bare walls, Griffith showed up. Like he needed him to be there to witness his shame.

"I just heard. I'm so sorry, my friend." Kip asked him what he'd heard. "You know what I've heard about this place. And before you ask, no, neither Danburn nor the others know. I've come to help you, if you'll allow it."

"They ruined it all." Griff, what he'd been calling him since they'd met, nodded and told him he was sorry again. "Yes, well, so will they be when I find them. Have you seen your brother again?"

"No, not since yesterday. He'd been by the house a couple of times before I brought Lilac home, apparently, I was out of town. But no, we've not spoken since yesterday. James is going

5

to be trouble, I think. That's not right—he is definitely going to be trouble. I don't understand him most of the time. I mean, why the fuck hasn't anyone taken him to task yet?" Kip asked him why he'd not done it either. "I can't. I made a promise to my mother that I'd not harm him. Then she revised that to I couldn't kill him after James killed my father. I don't want to do either, to be honest, but he's after something that belongs to me. I found her, Kip. Just before my brother would have killed her. He would have, too."

"I'm so glad that you've found your mate. And, so you know, I really like her too." He looked around the castle that had been in his family for several hundred generations. "They have been here too long, I think. I know that you're aware of my family situation, and I have to tell you, I'm ashamed to be related to them, especially my mother, in all this. Why couldn't we all have parents like Danburn does? But I guess we don't get to pick our relatives. I just want to get rid of all this and then start anew. I was just going to do that when you showed up."

"I'd gladly help you." Kip didn't want to be beholden to anyone, but of all the people he knew, Griff would be the most helpful and the kindest of anyone. "I can start on the upper levels and you at the bottom. We can meet in the middle and then start on the lawns around the place."

Kip told him that he was grateful for his help and made his way to the lower level. Kip felt the pull of his dragon and let him consume him. His dragon was much like Danburn in that he was several hundred times larger than his other self, but he wasn't nearly as strong as the king was. Spraying flames all over the sub flooring of his ancestral home, Kip watched as everything that had been left behind by his family was burned away. Good riddance to it all.

He thought about what he'd had to endure by living here

as a young dragon. Not just the hatred of his parents, but that of the town here as well. Few knew that he had spent his life living no more than a few leagues from Danburn, but even fewer knew that the inhabitants of the castle here were his parents and his siblings. And he liked it that way.

None of them had been happy that he'd been born and that he'd lived. He had an older brother and a sister that had had their lives pretty perfect, according to them, when he'd come into the world to upset their lives. Kip had no idea how they'd come to that conclusion, but they had made his life a living hell from the moment he'd been hatched. And had nearly killed him on several occasions.

But now they were all gone, and he hoped that they'd stay that way. He'd not heard from them nor seen them in more years than he could count, which by his estimation wasn't nearly long enough. Not to say that they were dead — Kip knew that it was only a matter of time before they'd return now that he was the sole owner of the family castle. What they didn't know was that he'd become much more powerful than any of them, even all together, due in part to his being on the good side of a dragon who was very powerful, not to mention the king of them all.

He was on the second level of the castle when he could see that the heat of the stone was burning things on this level too. His work was nearly finished here in cleaning things out. The real work, getting it back to its former glory, would take a great deal longer. But he was up for the task. He only hoped that in a few months, he felt the same way.

The walls of the castle would not crumble under the heat of his breath, but they would remain hot for a very long time. Since it had been created for a dragon and by one, it would not burn and fall under the heat of one. It was said that if a dragon were to heat a stone with his breath, it would be a decade or more before it would be cool enough to touch. He hoped in his case that it was true, and that it would be just hot enough to keep his family away. But he knew better.

Watching it all burn away with a kind of contentment that he'd not had in a while, he looked at Griff when he came toward him as his dragon. The two of them shifted and became themselves, basking in the heat they'd made as well as what they'd been able to do in such a short amount of time. Not that Kip couldn't have done it on his own, but having someone with him made his heartbreak better.

They looked to be a matched set of dragons, both of them as green as the grasses that had once been around the keep—but that was about as far as the similarity went. And, he thought, that was what had made them such good friends over the decades—opposites attracting. The two of them were perfect in that saying.

Kip was one to jump into a situation that might get him into trouble, and most of the time, that was the point. Griff was more cautious, and someone that never took chances that he didn't have to. Kip supposed it was because of his family, namely his brother. James had been a troublesome person since he'd been born and was forever taking chances on things that were better left alone. And having Griff around just made it clearer, to anyone who was around them for very long, just how horrific James was.

They were standing outside the castle walls when they sat down to watch the heat dance off the top of the turrets. It really wasn't much to see, not out here, but the glow and ebbing of the castle walls from hot to cooler was a beautiful sight to behold. Neither of them said much as the darkness spread over the lands, with only the lights from the stone in front of them to light the way. Kip asked Griff what he'd found out about James.

"He's been around hurting women again. And he had my mate for a time as well. He'd not raped her, thankfully for him, but she's been hurt. I have her at the house now, as safe as I can make her. But she doesn't trust that James and I are two different people yet, so I've introduced her to the staff and told her that I'd return. James now looks for her, thinking to take all that she has and make it his own before he kills her. Or before he would have tried to kill her." Kip had heard from others how sadistic James was. And that he never left a woman—or man, for that matter—in one piece if he had the time to make them suffer in horrific ways. "My mate, she's a faerie of some considerable age. But her magic has been depleted by trying her best to stay away from James and heal herself. Right now I have Bud working with her to get her wounds healed."

"Does James know that it was you who bought the family home?" Griff nodded with a large grin. "I wish I could have been there when you told him. I can only imagine what he had to say about that. I'm sure that he wasn't particularly nice about it."

"No, not even close to it. He wants me to give him money. Or gems. I told him that I wouldn't, thinking, and rightly so, that he'd only be back for more and more." Griff looked at the castle while he continued. "He killed our father and mother. I don't know how it happened with Mother, but Dad had his head removed, and James left him for the buzzards to feast on. Had I not come along, I have no idea what might have happened to his body."

Kip told him what he'd heard about James. It wasn't as if he'd been spying on him, but Griff had asked him to keep an eye out for him and anything that he might know of women he might have harmed. And there had been plenty over the

9

ensuing years. James was making quite a name for himself when it came to his murderous ways.

"There are four women that I know of for sure that he's killed. For two of them I've compensated their families, and the other two, their entire families were killed as well. I'm sorry to be the bearer of bad news, but he's wanted by the council as well. Why they've not found him yet is beyond me. It's not as if he is keeping himself hidden away." Griff nodded and told him that he'd pay Kip back for the other families. "No need for that, Griff. You would and have done the same for me. Not for a death, but in helping me get back up on my feet again."

"You're my friend, Kip. Forever and a day will you have a friend in me as well. But with James.... The council has contacted Danburn about him. He only came to me yesterday about it. I'm aware of James's misdeeds, but not all of it, apparently. He's been on a murderous streak for the last few months. And I've been given permission to take care of him in any way that I feel necessary." Kip whistled. "Yes, you can well imagine the ways to rid myself of him too. Except for the promise I made."

"Your mother, do you think he actually killed her? I mean, she was a very powerful dragon on her own. But she was also one of the founding women of the set of bylaws." Griff said that there was no other explanation for where she might have gone. Her body had disappeared. "Yes. There is a rumor that she was so heartbroken that she died just to be with her mate. There is a faerie garden that is hers and his as well. I have seen it."

"As have I. The faeries about, they've made sure that it hasn't been discovered by anyone with ill intentions. And yes, that would include James. Some think that he would rob their graves just to be able to take what doesn't belong to him." Kip knew that as well. "Did you know that he has made it his business to find where there are faerie gardens and destroy them? He doesn't even have to know the person there, he just destroys everything about it. I cannot believe at times that we're from the same parents. The only thing I can figure that's going to stop James is someone to kill him. But it can't be me."

"I know about blood promises, Griff. I myself had to promise that I'd not harm anyone in my family as well." But his promises were not made between him and his parents, but him and Danburn. And Kip was sure that if it came down to it, Danburn would allow him to do whatever was necessary to end their reign of terror.

Starting on the lawns as the sun was coming up around them, they burned most of it away because of the neglect. Kip thought about all the things he'd have to do to bring the house back to its former glory. First and foremost, he was going to find someone to help him with putting a ward on the place, to not only keep the vermin away, but his family as well. Laughing to himself, he thought they were just as much vermin as any other animals that could breach his home.

By the time daylight was fully making itself known to them, he and Griff had burned away all of the fallen trees and pulled what the brownies could use to one side. There wasn't as much as he'd hoped, but it was there for them to use however they wished. Kip owed a great deal to all the creatures of the lands.

~*~

Lilac woke up and looked around. The man, her mate, had brought her here several hours ago, and now that she was in a place that she could not only rest but also heal, and she wondered what he'd want in return. Everyone, to her anyway, wanted something for the smallest of deeds they did for you. This man, related to the horrid James, would be no better.

The door opened just as she was getting up, and she stared at the woman standing before her. Lilac dropped to the floor when she realized that she'd been rude in her greeting. The laughter that came from the beautiful woman had her peeking up to see what had been so funny.

"Please don't do that. It makes me feel silly, and I'm sure that having your bottom up in the air like that isn't the least bit comfortable for you either. I do envy you being able to do that, however. Feeling like an overgrown elephant doesn't give me the agility that I once had." Lilac glanced at her while sitting on her knees. "Come now — you've been hurt, and I don't stand on ceremony when you're family. And you are, as Griff's mate."

"I know his name, but I'm not going to be the mate to a sadistic bastard. If it's all the same to you, now that I'm better healed, I'll just leave." The woman, the queen of dragons, sat down on the chair that was by the bed. When asked to have a seat as well, Lilac wasn't sure what to do.

"Please, have a seat and we'll get to know each other." She had no choice but to sit on the side of the bed, trying her best to keep her head lower than the queen's. "Don't do that. Don't think that you are less than myself when I'd like nothing more than for us to be friends. What's your name? I forgot to ask Griff when he told us that you were here."

"I'm Lilac of the Water. My family dates back more years than could be counted by any human. You're the queen of dragons, mate to the king, Danburn." The woman laughed and told her she was, but for her to call her Kendrick. "I cannot do that, my lady. Even with you saying that you wish us to be friends, I'll not breach protocol and be so familiar with you."

"All right. For now, anyway. I've come to talk to you about Griff and his brother James. I wasn't even aware, to be honest, that he had a brother, much less a twin. I'm to understand that they look like the same person. And other than James being so heavy, there's no way you can tell them apart. However, from what I've been able to find out, that is where the resemblance ends. They're as different as night and day when it comes to temperament and kindness."

"So you say. I spent two days with James, and I can tell you that there is not another person like him, thankfully." Lilac watched the other woman and knew that she was breeding—the size of her belly made her think that she was close, too. She wondered if she knew that she was having a girl but didn't say anything—it wasn't any of her business. "The other man, he said that his name was Griffith. Is this his home? He told me that he was bringing me here to heal, but that's all I know."

"Yes. This is his home. And he's away right now helping Kip. Griff asked me to come by and see if you needed anything. And since he knows what you are, he's asked that I tell you that the lake nearby is there for you to use. Danburn had the lake made so that his dragon could swim in it without any troubles. It's very deep, from what I've been told. But I do know that it will hold his dragon, so you should have no problems with it."

"I will need to submerge myself to heal completely. What sort of tax will I need to pay to be able to use the king's lake? I have little money with me, and nothing to show for my life here on this earth." Kendrick told her that it was there for her to use. "For free? I doubt that you believe that either. Everyone wants something."

"Not here we don't. And especially not family. You're going to have to learn to trust us, Lilac. We have nothing but your goodwill in mind when we offer you something. I'm not sure why you're so hard on us when you've only just met us. However, I'd very much appreciate it if you didn't lump all of us in the same category as you have James." Her temper was showing, and Lilac had a feeling that it wasn't often that she lost it. "Now, we're going to get you dressed, unless you can do that on your own."

"I can. I have magic to keep myself safe." Kendrick nodded and stood up. "I don't want to be here, my lady. James will find me, and I will not subject myself to his kind of...to him at all."

"I don't know him, as I have said. But Danburn does, and his hatred of the man is enough for me to dislike him too. I know that James is around, and that he's not a dragon. But as far as what he's done, as I said, I don't know yet. There wasn't time for me to do a complete search of him and his trouble. But you can trust me to know that before he comes sniffing around here again. I'll be better prepared for his ass." Lilac didn't want to like this woman, didn't trust her either. But she had a feeling that she would get to the bottom of anything she set her mind to. "You should meet the staff here. I know that you've talked to Bud, but there are many more here that are excited to meet you."

"I have nothing to offer them." Kendrick asked her what she thought they'd need from her. "I don't know. A lady of the house? A person who might know how to have a staff? I've been on my own longer than you've been around. Not to say that I'm insulting you, never that. But I don't know how to be a proper lady to a house like this. Nor to a man such as Griff. I'm just a faerie."

"Just a faerie? I don't know you well yet, but I have a feeling that you are no more just a faerie than I am just a woman." Lilac dressed, taking her cues from the other woman, in jeans and a large T-shirt. No shoes, however. Lilac didn't care for them. "Now, I've heard from Griff. He's on his way back here from helping Kip. Griff also said that he's not seen James around, so you might be all right to venture out if you wish, but not too far. I guess he no more trusts James than you do."

"He tried to rape me. James did, I mean. He's not a person

that I'd be around at all if I could help it. You should also take it easy. He'll harm you and your child if given the chance." Kendrick turned to look at her as they were going down the stairs. "It was more than that, a great deal more, but I knew that as soon as he was finished with me, he'd murder me. That day wasn't one of the days when I'd gladly have that happen."

"You've wished to die other times though?" Lilac saw no reason to lie to her, not that she could anyway, so she nodded at her. "I see. And this day, is it a good day or one that I have to watch out for you?"

"I don't appreciate you making fun of me. I don't want to be around most days. It's difficult to be what I am and have to deal with the shit that comes along all the time." Kendrick said nothing. "I need to get out of here. I don't want to be here any longer than I have to be."

"I'm sorry that you thought I was mocking you. I wasn't. I can understand completely how down you can be. I was for most of my life before meeting Danburn. I had a sister and a mother that were as bad, I think, as James is. My mother shot me in the head and left me for dead, and then couldn't understand why I wouldn't help her and Louise when I was put in foster care to heal." Lilac felt terrible for being so short with her and said as much. "It's all right. How would you have known? But you have to trust me when I tell you that we're all here for you. All of us."

"To what point? I mean, what will you want from me in exchange? I have nothing, as I have said, but my magic. And while it's considerable, it's not much in comparison to what dragons might have. Especially dragons that are the king and queen of their kind." Lilac went down the rest of the stairs and turned to look at the younger woman. "I'm afraid that whatever Griff might want from me, I won't submit to him. I'm my own

15

person, and he'll have to deal with that."

"I have no idea what this conversation is about, but you'll never have to submit to anything that you don't wish to. I'm not my brother." Lilac turned to look at the man as he stood in the doorway to the other part of the house. "My name is Griffith Alexander Farley, the fourth Earl of Alexander's Folly. The Duke of Winebarger and Baron of Windemere Castle. I'm a dragon of good standing and always have been. I'm not my brother."

"So you say. But how would I know that?" She felt rather than saw Kendrick leave them, but Lilac wanted to make a point and it wasn't going to be nice. "You have a lot of titles and seem to be very proud of them. However, you'll find that I couldn't care less what you have attached to your name. I only care what you think you're going to be doing to me."

"Do to you? Why, nothing that you don't want. As I have said to you repeatedly, I'm not James. He's a sadistic fuck that I have hated most of my life. He killed my parents without regard to what they were to us, simply because he could. He has murdered and taken anything that he wanted since we were children. He thought that as the first born, by only mere minutes before me, that he should have anything and everything that he wanted. And if he didn't get it in a conventional way, he'd take it, killing whatever got into his way when he did." He took several steps toward her, and Lilac lifted her chin and didn't move. "I've spoken to him about you. Or he has told me that you're his mate and that you've escaped. He has no idea that you're here, and this household will make sure that he doesn't."

"You're the second born? And you're a dragon? How did that happen? He should have been given your parents' all. No matter what he is." Griff told her that he didn't know, but perhaps the fates knew what sort of person James would turn

16

out to be. "Perhaps. But I still don't trust you. And more than likely never will. I'm very sorry for that. But I want you to know from the start my feelings on this. I might be your mate and I may have to stay here, but you'll never own my heart. Nor my body, even if you use it."

He pulled her body to his. His grip was tight, but not painful. It was like he was possessing her in some way. When he said her name, gently, like a caress, she put her hands to his chest to push him away. But touching him, she could feel his heat, his magic, as it blanketed over her like the sun did when she had a chance to be out in it in the early morning.

"I have no wish, none at all, to take anything that you aren't willing to part with. That would include your body." She struggled, and he held her tighter. Lilac could feel his erection and stopped moving. "My body is reacting to how lovely you are. That you belong to us, my dragon and me. But there isn't any way that I'd take from you, not with your heart as broken as it is. I promise you this, Lilac. You're as safe with me as you would be with your own mother, if she is as kind as you are."

He let her go and took a step back. Lilac was slightly unsteady on her feet, but held onto the table that was just behind her. Watching him, she could see the struggle he was having too. Whether it was from wanting to take her, his anger, or something else, she couldn't tell. But when he turned and made his way back the way he'd come, Lilac held tighter to the table so that she'd not fall on her face.

"Christ." That about summed it up, she thought. She was mated to a dragon — a very strong and old one. And his brother was out there, trying his best to take her and then kill her.

Lilac sat down on the floor and called out to her own faerie. Sunny came to her immediately. She needed the strength that the small faerie would give her and closed her eyes when her

17

magic healed all her wounds but the deeper cut on her leg. It was painful, but not nearly as much as her heart was broken right now.

She thought about leaving—just disappearing into the outside and hoping no one would find her. But she also knew that once she left there, Griff would find her. And while she didn't think that he'd hurt her for leaving, she just didn't know. He was, as she thought, a dragon with considerable strength, and not one to fuck with.

Getting up, she made her way in the direction that Griff had taken. It led her right to the kitchen, the heart and soul of any home that a dragon had. Sitting down when she was asked, a large platter of greens and flowers was set in front of her. Griff was having a sandwich as large as her arm, and a salad as well. Picking up the fork to fortify herself with her meal, she kept a careful eye on her host.

Lilac didn't smell poisons or any other kind of mixture to make her ill, but she was very cautious as to what she put in her mouth. The salad was good, just the right mixture of different greens with a beautiful array of edible flowers. It wasn't until she was finished that she realized that he was staring at her. Pushing her plate away, she stared right back.

"I've some news if you'd like it." Lilac asked him what it was about. "You and James. Mostly him and what he's saying about you. He is spreading the word that you're his mate and that the two of you had a tiff—his words, not mine. No one is saying anything. Not that they knew you were here, but Danburn is making sure that everyone knows that James is trouble and they shouldn't interact with him. Also, he's asked that everyone go around in pairs or more so as not to be a target before he can be caught. I'm to understand from some of his other victims' families that it matters little to him whether you're male or female."

"That's right. If he's around, why is no one catching him? It would seem to me that this is an easy catch. Or am I wrong about that?" He said that she wasn't. "Then why is he still on the streets?"

"He's not a dragon." She started to ask him what the hell that meant when it occurred to her. "I can see by your face that you get it. There is not one group that wants to take responsibility for his actions. The dragon council knows that he is the son of a dragon, but he's not one. The paranormal council won't touch him for the same reasons. Everyone wants him put away, but no one wants to do it. I call that lazy, but then that's just me."

"And what happens when he kills again? Will someone step in then?" Griff shrugged. "You don't care if he kills again, or you don't care who takes him away? I know that he's your brother. Is that the reason why he's still out there terrorizing people?"

"I care very much if he kills again. But I cannot, for personal reasons, do anything about it. And I washed my hands of James long ago. Just after our mother was presumed dead by his hand. Would I like to have him killed? Yes, with all my heart." Lilac asked him what had happened to his mother. "My mother was fed iron every day for several weeks. He admitted that, in addition to admitting that he killed our father. James removed our father's head one afternoon when our father refused to turn the family fortune over to him. As you can well imagine, he's not welcome around here or anywhere that he might put his hat."

Lilac started to tell him that she'd gladly kill James when Griff suddenly stood up. She did as well and waited for him to tell her what was going on. As he rushed to the door, he told her not to leave the house, that James was nearby. Sitting back down, she had to wonder what James had done now.

Chapter 2

Griff wasn't really mad, but he wasn't thrilled either. There were things going on that he wished he could have a part in, but couldn't because James was his brother. Most of it was things that he really didn't want to get involved in anyway. He looked over at Danburn when he said his name, probably not for the first time.

"Are you all right with this?" His face heated up in embarrassment when he told him that he hadn't been paying attention. "Yes, I kind of got that when you zoned out on us. I wanted to know what your take is on the councils, both of them, getting involved with this. Do you have a problem with James being arrested?"

"No. I mean, if anyone needs to be put behind bars, it would be him. Don't you think?" Danburn nodded. "I am worried that he'll figure out that I have Lilac at my house. And while I know that she can more than likely come out on top against him, I worry that he won't fight fair and he'll hurt her. Then I'll have to kill him. I should have already."

"Yes. I agree with you there. Someone should have by now.

21

Do you have any idea why your mom disappeared when she did?" He looked at Danburn and said that she'd been killed. "No, I don't think so. At least from what I've gathered about this. Her body would have reverted to her human self if she had been a dragon when she was killed. But, if she'd been killed with iron while a human, she wouldn't have had the strength to have turned into a dragon to leave. The poisons would have made her weak, had your brother actually fed her enough iron to have killed her. But you know as well as I that it would take a great deal of iron to have killed a dragon as large as she was."

"I don't understand. Are you saying that my mother might be out there somewhere? Waiting on what? For James to be killed? Or to see if I kill him." Danburn said that he didn't know for sure, but that's what he'd heard from Quinn. "She's been reading up on it for me?"

"She's been given all the dragon books, so I guess in a way, she's been looking for you. I'm to understand that he fed her iron in some of her meals, correct?" Griff nodded. "You know as well as I do that it wouldn't kill her. Not unless he had given it to her over a twenty or thirty-year timeframe. As it was, you thought it was only a few weeks after your father was killed that she disappeared. That isn't enough time for it to have killed her. Not in the small doses that he would have been feeding her. Also, if it had been much more than just a little, she would have been able to smell it."

"I never.... My father had only been dead for a few weeks when she was considered dead." Griff started pacing the room. If he was honest with himself, he was having a hard time thinking of anything but the woman in his home. Their home. "Why do you think she's still hiding out if she is alive?"

"I would imagine for the same reasons that you said. Because James is still out there. I'd certainly hide out if I were her. Wouldn't you?" Griff nodded and paced some more, his mind a whirl of activity from trying to think. "Griff, if he didn't kill her, then the dragon council will not be able to take him to task. And as you have no proof that he killed your father, then the paranormal council's hands will be tied too."

"Christ, this is a nightmare."

He stood by the office door and looked out over the work that was being done to his backyard. Danburn had caught him in the middle of working, but he had been glad for the interruption. Griff wasn't sure how much he'd been getting done anyway. He had a distraction much larger than his brother at the moment.

Griff looked at Danburn when he spoke again.

"He's been going around town telling anyone that will listen that you cheated him out of his inheritance. And that he is going to rule the castle now that someone has cleaned it up for him. I'm assuming that you've taken care that he can't return there." Griff nodded. "I have someone doing a search on your mom. But before he goes too far into it, I wanted to ask you if you care whether or not she's found."

"Yes. We were good together. The three of us—my father, my mother, and me. James considered himself above whatever activities we were doing. Even taking trips, he was too busy to join us." He thought of his brother and what he'd been like even as a child. "When we'd return from wherever we'd been, he would bitch and groan about how we'd left him behind and how we'd not brought him anything home. Like he was a four-year-old or something. Once, when we'd been gone for nearly a month, the castle was in shambles when we returned. Mom and Dad were so upset about it, and more so when he told them that they should have known better than to leave him unattended for so long. The fucker made it sound like it was their fault that he was a grown man and couldn't be trusted at home alone."

"I'm sorry, Griff. I knew that it was bad at your home, but I had no idea what had happened to your family." He waved him off, not wanting him to give him sympathy. "What do you plan to do when he comes back? You know as well as I do that he will."

"I don't know. If my mom is out there, I could ask her to take away this promise I made to her. It's the only way that I can think of to end his reign of terror. Especially since everyone's hands are tied." He thought of Lilac and what she'd told him yesterday. "My mate would gladly end his life after what he did to her. He had her tied to a tree naked. And had it not been for her faeries, she might well have been there when he returned. I don't even want to think about what he would have done to her then."

Griff watched the rain falling. It was needed, the rain, but it was also somewhat sad to him as well. It was dreary and wet. It was only a few days until the Fourth, and closer to when Kendrick was to have her child. He looked over at Danburn and asked him if he was ready to be a father. Griff laughed when he seemed to light up with the question.

"I am. We've put together all the furniture and things that we bought. Also, a rocker like the one that my mom had when I was a baby has been cleaned and refinished. Kendrick just loves it." He asked him if they were ready for the ceremony. "Oh yes. Mom is taking care of it for us. She said that it was her pleasure to do so. I think she just wants to be the first to hold the baby, but she has been getting things set up."

The ceremony of welcoming a baby into the family was something older than both of them. The child would be born, and would be marked by its father then its mother. After that, he or she would be presented to friends and the rest of the family, each of them bestowing a gift to the child fitting with their future status as a royal. Then rest of the household would meet the child.

There was more to it than that, but Griff was actually looking forward to the celebration. It would last an entire month, having the young child on display for all to come by and pay homage to. He had already gotten his gift for the baby, as well as one for Kendrick and Danburn.

Griff was worried a little about James coming around and spoiling things for Danburn. He knew, as did the rest of their crew, that James hated them all, especially Danburn. He'd always been jealous of his wealth, as well as his titles. He'd called him Damn Bird all his life, but only behind his back. Griff had taken great pleasure in telling Danburn what his brother called him. And he'd come up with a suitable nickname for him as well — Jiminy Cricket. James hated that as much as Danburn had thought it was funny about his name.

"Tell me what you want me to do, Griff, and you know that I'll do it. We've been friends for far too long for us to stand on ceremony about your troubles. All of us will be here for you."

Griff started to tell him that he had no idea what he wanted when Lilac came into the room.

Danburn stood up and bowed before her, and Griff watched her face to see how she would react. Both of them knew what sort of faerie she was — a water faerie. But neither of them knew what sort of lineage she had. Lilac could be any one of a thousand faeries. Whatever she was, it mattered little to him — he would still protect her with his life.

"You're a water faerie." Lilac nodded at Danburn and looked at Griff before sitting down on the little sofa in his office. "It's been a very long time since I've seen one of your kind. I know that there are more, but I had no idea that any were this

25

close to us."

"I wasn't around here until that idiot brother of his tried to kill me. He needs to be put down like the animal that he is." He and Danburn agreed with her. "Then why is he still walking around like he owns the world? I would have thought by now someone would have killed him. Had I been at full strength when he caught up with me, we'd not be having this conversation."

"A blood promise made on a deathbed prevents me from taking him out. And I would have loved to even before he harmed you." Lilac glanced at him and asked him who the promise was made to. "My mother. She made me promise that I'd never harm him. It wasn't until right before she disappeared that she revised it to not kill him. I took that to mean that I could harm him, just not finish him off. Until recently, he's not been around where I was. But now that he is, I plan on making him wish that he'd never come around here."

"I see." She stood up and looked at the wound on her leg. It wasn't healing the way that it should have after getting help from her faerie. Griff had thought them all healed, but it wasn't until she started pacing that he realized this one hadn't. He was just about to suggest that she go with him to the lake that Danburn created when she turned to him again. "I'm not very trusting. I'm sure that you've figured that out. Nor am I going to be an easy lay for you. I might be your mate, but I neither trust you to not hurt me, nor that when you have me, you'll not turn me over to James. I know that it's not fair of me to say that, or to even think that, but I'm not going to lie to you. And I'd appreciate it if you didn't lie to me either. And omission is the same as a lie to me."

"It is for me as well. But I can only tell you what I know for sure. I won't keep things from you, even at the cost of hurting your feelings. I would rather have all the information up front than to go into battle and not know it all." Lilac nodded and looked at Danburn. He introduced the two of them. "Not only is he the king of dragons, but he is also my dearest friend. You'll meet the rest of them soon."

"Do you have any questions for me, my lady?" She shook her head at Danburn, then nodded. "I, too, will not lie to you, either by fib or omission. But you must be prepared to have any of us be truthful to the point of bluntness. When you meet the rest of the women in this family, you'll understand that more."

"I know your mother." Danburn said that she'd told him that. "She was one of the dragons that came to our village when it had been overrun by pirates. The pirates killed a great many of us; my parents and siblings were some of the few who escaped. But the dragons helped us by burning down the destroyed huts, as well as burying the dead. I don't know what we would have done without them. They even provided us with food and water to care for those that had been hurt."

"Mother is here. She'd been on a holiday until recently. She's home for the birth of my child. You'll be there too, will you not?" Lilac didn't answer him, but she did look at Griff. "Griff is going to be her godfather, and I would wish that you'd be her godmother, now that you're a part of this family."

"I don't want to be here." Danburn said that he knew that as well. "If James comes around again, he might want to hurt you or your family. It would be best if I made my way back to my home and don't tempt him into coming here. I have a feeling that he doesn't like to be told no, nor to have his plans thwarted."

"No, he does not." Griff sat down on the couch with her but not close enough to touch her. Not yet. "James is going to be in for a rude awakening if he thinks that you're going to be an easy catch for him. And I will be by your side when you teach him whatever lessons you wish."

"I wish for him to be dead. He has the blood of a great many people on his hands. They're stained with it." Griff told her he agreed. "Yes, you would. And this blood promise that you made, you're going to hold it, correct? Even if it's me that he hurts again?"

"Nay, he will be dead before he is able to touch you. Promise or not, I will tear him apart and think nothing more about it if he so much as breaks your nails. You are my mate, and I will protect you with my life."

~*~

Lilac had to admit, she did dearly love the house. It was large, homey, and had a great deal of touches that made her think that the man who lived here had tastes that reflected her own. Making her way to the solarium, she marveled at the array of plants there. Not only were there herbs and flowers, but also tiny trees just waiting to be put into the earth to grow up to be just as their sire was.

"Miss, if there is anything that you wish to have here, you tell me and we'll bring it here. The master of the house, he is just getting things started, but the faeries and brownies about, they've been helping them grow." Lilac said that she loved this room. "As do I. My name is Hoke. I'm the gardener here. And I come in here to dabble a bit when I have the time. I've been working with the trees in here, and as you can see, they're coming along nicely."

"I can see that. They're going to be strong trees soon." She touched her finger to the oak tree sapling that was nearest to her. "I have some seeds that are all but gone from around here. I will have them brought to you soon, if you'd like."

"Yes, that would be very nice. Does the tree tell you if it

needs anything?" Lilac looked at Hoke. "I know what you are, miss. And if you can tell me how we're making our way, the trees and myself, I'd be very grateful. As I said, I'm only dabbling here."

"They're doing well. A little more sunlight would be the only thing that they're needing. But as I said, they're doing well under your care." She moved to the flowers that were some of the ones that she'd had for her salad last night. "How long have you worked for Griff, Lord Farley? You have things established here very well, so a while now, I'm guessing."

"Yes, for some decades. These plants, most were here, overgrown with weeds when I was asked to come and take care of this for him. Lord Farley, he's a good man. Nothing like his brother James. I'm to understand that you've had a run in with the other man." She nodded but said nothing. "He's a monster, and Lord Farley knows it. Their mother, she tied up his hands in dealing with him too. Why, just a few years ago, James killed a woman and tried to blame it on Lord Farley. Took them several days to sort that one out. But for some reason, James was never brought in for the murder. The household here, they'd like nothing better than to see him put in irons."

"He told me, Lord Farley, that he was nothing like his brother. I'm beginning to see that he's not." Hoke gave a smile that seemed to touch every part of his body. "You like your lord, I take it."

"Oh yes, my lady. We all do. He's been a good man to work for—and with, I might add. When we moved here, the household, he made sure that we had everything that we needed. He even set it up so that our families had a place to lay their heads at night if they wanted to come." Lilac told Hoke that she was just getting to know the master of the house. "You'd do no better than having one such as him as your mate, if you don't mind me saying so. He's honest and kind, but he can also be ruthless when the need arises."

She'd seen neither of those sides of him. It wasn't like there was anything going on right now to warrant such a behavior as him being ruthless, but she had a feeling that it was going to come to that with his brother. Or, and this was what she actually thought would happen, he'd turn her over to him and not care a whit what became of her. Lilac nodded when Hoke said that he'd be back later.

Lilac wandered around the plants, some of them as big, if not bigger than she was. They were tropical plants and enjoyed the heat that was here for them. Rounding the last of the tables set up for holding new plants, she saw Griff standing there watching her.

"I'm not touching anything." She had no idea why she'd said that and told him she was sorry. "I've been off for a while now, and I'm sorry to have taken it out on you."

"I know how you feel. My brother is causing trouble enough for the two of us. Hoke said that you were in here. I came to see if you would like to go into town with me. I have a few stops to make before the end of the day, and I wanted to be with you." She asked him why. "Why do I want to be with you? Well, I like the way you smell. The way you look when you think no one is looking. The sad smiles that you have, as if you'd only just thought of something that happened long ago. If you're asking me what I have to do in town, then I'll tell you that I have to see a man about a horse. Quite literally. He has a harras that he is willing to sell me. Hoke explained to me that we need the horse shit. I actually thought he was kidding, but he does need it."

"Fertilizer." Griff smiled and said that was it. "What of your brother? Do you plan to hand me over to him as soon as you see him?"

Griff moved across the floor so fast that she didn't realize it until he was holding her. Her body fit his, was all she could think about. He was big, a very large man both in height and girth. But he wasn't fat. Nor did he hold her to him like he meant any harm to her. Looking up at him, she could see his anger, but had a feeling that it wasn't entirely directed at her. She asked him what had happened. He touched his head to hers and she could feel his sorrow like her own.

"James killed a woman last night. She looked a great deal like you, and it terrified me when I thought it was you." She felt every emotion as it ran over his body. "I would never turn you over to him. Not even under threat of death, or for any other reason. You're mine. And I am yours. Forever and a day. Understand?"

Nodding, she reached up and touched her fingers to his cheek. He looked hard, but his skin was soft; the bristle of beard that was there felt unfamiliar to her touch. Opening her palm over his face, she could feel his struggle—at what she could only guess, but she wasn't sure if she really wanted to know. When he lowered his mouth to hers, it was the most natural thing in the world to her to wrap her hand around his neck and pull him the scant few inches to her mouth.

His moan made her dizzy. Griff's touch made her want to be closer to him, to feel his flesh against hers. As the kiss deepened, he pulled her tighter to him and this time she moaned, her entire being on fire now for him. When he lifted his head, she looked into his eyes and saw another fight going on in them. She watched him as he pulled away from her, yet held her to him.

"I want you, Lilac. Very much so. But I don't want you to regret coming to me either." She nodded, unsure what he was saying. Did he not want her? "With all that I am, I want you.

31

But you need to say the words to me. I don't want to take what isn't freely given to me."

"I don't know what I want, Griff." He nodded, but still held her in his arms. "I've never wanted to belong to anyone. Not just you. I don't want to become lost in a man."

She felt the loss of his warmth when he let her go and stepped back. Her body cooled so quickly and so profoundly when he moved back that she wanted to reach for him again. But when he took another step back from her, Lilac knew that he was not being selfish — he was giving her the opportunity to tell him yes or no.

"I'm going into town to see about the horses. Would you like to come with me? James will not touch you." He said it so that it left her little doubt that James would die if he tried anything. Nodding to him, he smiled. "Good. I've a few other places to run to as well. If you get bored with them, Quinn said that you could hang out with her at the restaurant."

Getting into his truck with him, she looked at the massive barn that was back from the garage. There were so many outbuildings here. Most of them were in good shape, but the barn needed of a lot of work, she could see. Lilac knew that the smaller faeries could do whatever repairs needed to be done on it for nothing but a few flowers, and would enjoy the work too. Reaching out to one that she knew the most and who had a large pip that worked with him, she asked Sanders if he would like to take it on.

Oh, my lady, I've heard that you have yourself a mate. A fine one at that. Congratulations on that. He's been helping us around here since he bought yonder house. He's even put out sugar and water for us to use whenever we wish. Lord Griffith is a good man. One I would have chosen for you myself. Sanders could get off course in conversations better than anyone she knew. Keeping him focused on the one she was having, Lilac reminded him of what she'd asked. *Yes, the barn. We can do that. Lord Griffith, he's given us permission to look over the yards and tell him what needs to be repaired. I'm sure that it would be nothing for us to fix it up for you both.*

That would be nice of you, Sanders. Will you need his permission? Also, if you'd be so kind as to have Sunny working with you, she can keep me updated on things you might need. Sanders told her that he'd not asked, but thought it a good idea. He also said that he'd be glad to work with Sunny. *I'm with him now. I'll ask him and get back to you.*

Thank you, my lady. And again, I wanted to tell you how glad that we all are that you're his mate. The two of you, you've done great things for my kind. I can only imagine what you will do for us as a pair.

Lilac thanked him again and turned to Griff. "I have a few faerie friends that would like to work with you on the barn." Griff looked at her for a moment, then turned back to the road as he drove. "They'd like to redo it for you, for your kindness."

"I'm assuming that you know Sanders." She told him that she did. "He's the most exasperating man I've ever had to talk to. He is easily sidetracked, isn't he?"

Lilac laughed when he did. But he did give them permission to take care of the barn. Telling Sanders that Griff had given them permission to work, Lilac relaxed. Griff drove with ease, something that she'd never learned to do, and he was careful of stop signs and the such while he talked to her about what his plans were for the other two outbuildings on his property.

"I have an idea that I'd like to use the smaller of the two to put in a studio. At one time I was a potter. As you can imagine, being around for so long, I got pretty good at it. I've not been as productive as I should be. Not just with being a potter, but life

33

in general. I've become lazy, I guess you could say." She asked him why that was. "I didn't really have any set goals in mind, I think. I was floating along on my ass, not involving myself in even my own life. But with you here, I'd like to be — well, better. More active in my life."

"You don't have to do anything because of me. I don't care if you work or not. I'm sure, like me, you don't have to work to keep your standards of living up." He grinned at her and her face heated. "What I mean is, you don't have to impress me with anything. You're all right the way that you are."

That didn't come out right either. But when he laughed, Lilac found that she didn't care. His laughter was beautiful, if one could say that about laughing. And when she laughed with him, Lilac realized that she'd not done that in a long while. She felt better than she had in years, more like decades, just laughing with this man.

Chapter 3

James wasn't able to get into his family home, which sucked since he knew that somewhere in it there were enough gems to set him up for a while. The fucker, Griffith, lord of everything he wanted, had done just what James thought he would and made it so that he couldn't enter his own home. He'd fucking owned it until his brother had stepped in, taking over as he did everything that James did.

"One of these days he's going to get his comeuppance. See if he doesn't."

Returning to the area where Griffith lived, he decided to look him up. It was high time that the two of them had this out. He was sick to death of having to hold onto his coattails for every little thing he wanted. "Damned bastard won't even give a few gems to his own fucking brother."

Not that James thought that he deserved them. Even he knew that Griff didn't owe him anything. But he should want to take care of him. It was his duty to do so. Laughing, he thought of what Griffith would say if he said that to him. That it was his duty. Since they were small children, Griffith had never

35

once come to his aid in anything. And James hadn't helped him either. Nor would he ever.

Walking along the sidewalk, thinking of all the shit that had befallen him in the last decade or so, James knew that everything was his fault. He didn't care so long as he was happy with what came along, but he'd had money then. Now he didn't have shit, not even a safe place to sleep any longer. The grand that he'd had before coming to town to get more was gone. And he couldn't even remember what he'd spent it on.

He'd tried to be thrifty with it, not spend it on too many things that he really didn't need or want. But there had been a few things that he felt would make him look better to the women. Not that he really cared if they liked what he wore, but having nice clothing made them forget who he was for a moment. And that was all it took for him to get them. That had worked out well for him, but now that his fun was over, he didn't have even the pretties any longer.

The large van had been very nice. Getting the women to join him in it had worked well too. He'd made himself appear as an older woman, at times, who was having car trouble. After getting them close enough to where he wanted them, James had knocked them on the head and shoved them in the back.

When he had three of them back there, he drove them out to the property that the *king* owned and had his kind of fun with them. Dumping them on Damn Bird's land had been an extra bonus for him. James had hoped that the king would be blamed for their deaths, and had gone the extra mile, as he called it, in making them look like they'd been torn apart by the other man. But that hadn't worked either.

"The bastard must have everyone in his pockets is all I can figure."

James was tripped up on one of the broken sidewalks and

fell against the building. Just as he was going to go in and kill the man whose building was such a hazard, he saw his brother in a brand new truck parking across the street from him.

Griffith got out and moved to the other side of the truck and helped someone out. It took him several seconds to realize that it was that woman, the one that had gotten away. Moving to cross the street to confront Griffith, he nearly got himself run over when he didn't check the street before walking out into it. Of course Griffith turned and looked at him when the driver of the car laid on his horn as a warning. James knew that a sneak attack was out of the question then.

The woman was his. He recognized her as soon as she was helped from the truck by Griffith. When he got to the two of them, Griffith actually pushed the woman behind him, James's woman, like he owned her or something.

"You have my property, brother dear. I would like for you to hand her over before I have to hurt you." Griffith only cocked his perfect brow at him. "Hand her over and there won't have to be bloodshed. Now, I have no tolerance for this kind of shit. Give her to me. I found her first."

"She's my mate." He looked at the woman, who was glaring at him over Griffith's shoulder, and then back at his brother. "And as for bloodshed, you touch her and I don't care what Mother said at all—I will kill you where you stand. Move on, James. She's not going to come to you, ever, so long as I have breath in my body."

"I can take care of that for you, should you wish. I'd like nothing better than to have you dead. Give her to me." Griffith said nothing to him, nor did he give him the woman. Christ, she was beautiful. More so than he remembered her to be. "Griffith, am I going to have to go to the council about this? You know as well as I do that she's not your mate. You're just doing this to piss me off. If you don't want any trouble from me, just move and I'll be on my way with her. She's mine."

"No, I'm not going anywhere with you."

He wanted to shut her up, kill her, and drew back his fist to do so. As his hand was sailing toward her mouth, he was already feeling the satisfaction of hitting her when his hand was captured in Griffith's. The pain radiated up his arm and down to his belly. James heard his bones break as Griffith squeezed his hand in his. Not only could he not jerk from his brother's grip, but he was sure that if he tried very hard, he'd just pull his hand from his arm and toss it away. Going to his knees because of the pain, he heard the woman laughing. Then Griffith. Looking up at them both, he started cursing in every language he knew, just to make a point as to how much smarter he was than his brother. Right now it was all he had.

James was sick with the pain. The sound of his bones mashing together made him realize that Griffith was hurting him, but not with all his strength. Had he been doing so, he was sure that his hand would have broken off and he'd leave him there to bleed to death. So James did the only thing he could think of — he begged his brother to let him go.

When he released him, James cradled his shattered hand with the other hand. It was sickening to see it limply at the end of his wrist, the way that the bones stuck out of his flesh. He stood, wanting to hit his brother for hurting him unjustly, but he had to puke up his lunch. When James tried to straighten his finger out the pain intensified at that moment and he saw the earth move under him, his eyes crossing from the agony. When he fell to the ground, no longer able to stay upright, he laid there while his woman and brother stepped over him and moved away.

James had no idea how long he lay there. People walked

around him, never asking if they could assist him. He was sick several more times, each time that he accidently touched his hand or it moved a little too quickly. He cried a little too, unable to make the pain go away, and no matter how many times he tried to heal his broken hand, nothing would come of it. It was like with touching him like he had, Griffith had put a spell over him so that his ability to heal was taken from him. That would be so like him to do something like that.

When he was able to sit up, James carefully held his hand to him and walked to where he'd hidden his car. He wasn't sure that he could drive it should he need to, but he needed to get help. Going to the local clinic was all he could think of, and he made his way there. James was sweating like he'd run a marathon or two by the time he was standing inside the little offices. And the pain wasn't lessening like he thought it should have by now.

"I need help." The woman at the front desk looked familiar, but he wasn't in the mood to try and figure out who she was or where he'd seen her before. "Get up off your lazy ass and find someone to help me. Christ, can't you see that I'm in a great deal of pain?"

"Yes, I can see that you might hurt a little. Frankly, whatever happened to you, I'm sure that you deserved it." He just stared at the bitch with his mouth open. No one talked to him that way. "Go over there and sit down. When the doctor is ready to see you, Mr. Farley, he'll call out your number. And you'd better be nice, or you'll be out on your ass so quickly that the pain in your hand will seem minor when I'm finished with you."

He moved to where she'd told him to. James wasn't used to people talking to him that way. But in this, he was going to keep his mouth shut. If he didn't get help, and soon, he was going to have to live with this the rest of his days. And that

39

wasn't going to fucking happen.

While he was biding his time, waiting on his name to be called, he thought of what his woman was doing with his brother. His mate? Could she have been his mate? He would guess not. It had been too long for him to be getting his mate this late in his life. Besides, he'd seen her first, damn it. And as he was older than Griffith, he should be happy to have him take his mate first. But as he'd never been happy with anything he did, James didn't believe he would be in this either.

When his name was called an hour later, he went to the little cubical and told her that he wanted someone to fix his hand. Nodding, she told him that she was just for the insurance claims if he had any.

"Insurance claims. What the fuck is that? I just want one of the morons here to have a look at my hand and to fix it. I don't have any insurance." She told him that they had to figure out how much assistance he might need with his income. "I don't have an income. I'm far better than you are, so I don't need a job to pay for things. Send the bill to my brother, Griffith. He's the one that hurt me anyway."

"Griffith Farley is your brother?" James nodded and said that he was his younger brother. But he noticed that her entire demeanor changed when he told her who he was. "Then you'll have to pay for services before anyone will look at you. Let me find out how much to charge you. We cannot send the bills to anyone else, either—we all know what sort of person you are."

When she returned, James had his speech ready to blast her with. She wasn't going to treat him like this and get away with it. But when she sat down, he noticed that there were three very large burly men in the little office with them. He knew that she'd called in reinforcements, and that didn't make him any happier.

"The total of your billing will be two thousand eight hundred dollars. If it's over that, you'll be responsible for paying that too in a timely manner." She glared at him, and he could almost feel her hatred of him. "That will cover x-rays and a casting of your hand if it is indeed broken. Then there is the added cost of—"

"*If* it's broken? Listen, bitch, I don't have a medical degree, but even I can see that it's broken. Broken to fuck, if you ask me. I want you to call one of them doctors up here and tell them to fix this, or I'll come after them when they least expect it."

One of the men put his hands on his shoulders and James jerked around, but hit his hand on the desk before he could give the fucker a piece of his mind.

Christ, it was as if he was being crushed again. Screaming out in pain, he nearly passed out when he was lifted up and taken out of the room. As he sat back out in the waiting room again with the losers, he whimpered and cursed at his fucking bad luck today. Someone was going to pay for this shit, and at the top of the list was his brother and that fucking cunt that he claimed was his mate.

It was several more hours before anyone came to call his name again. By now James was in so much pain that he knew he had to keep his mouth shut. Fuck, but he wanted to murder someone—a lot of someones, as a matter of fact. But he knew that should he start spouting off again they'd throw him to the curb, and right on his sore hand.

The doctor said that he'd do some x-rays even before he touched him. But just as he was being wheeled back to wherever the fuck they were taking him, the bitch from the front desk came back and spoke to the doctor, telling the man that not only hadn't he paid, but he'd also insulted her. Before he knew it, James was out on the street with nothing more than a fucking

41

bill that he had no intention of paying. They had charged him eighty-four dollars to have some doctor throw him out of the stupid place.

James was hurting badly by the time he got back to his abandoned hotel room. There wasn't any electricity or hot water, but it was a place he could stay in without having anyone come up on him and hurt him more.

Laying on the three stacked up mattresses he'd brought in here days ago, James tried to will the pain away. He knew that eventually he'd heal, but it would take him days. Unlike Griffith, who would heal right up in a matter of seconds, James took much longer. Another thing to be fucking pissed about was how he'd gotten the shitty hand in this deal as well.

Closing his eyes, hoping that the pain would simply go away, James tried to distance himself from the agony by thinking of ways he was going to take care of Griffith and the woman. He wished now that he'd gotten her name. It would have been nice to have it to curse her out. As it was, that woman was all he could come up with.

"Griffith is going to pay for this. I don't know how or when, but he'll pay for this ill treatment of me." James nearly sobbed when the light sheet he'd pulled over himself laid over his hand. "Mother fucker, you're going to pay dearly for this."

He finally fell into a fitful sleep well after the sun came up the next morning. James had to do something, or he was going to explode. Not really explode himself, but his temper would. And he thought that was just what his brother needed. For him to lose his shit and take it all out on him. That'll show Griffith who the bigger man was. Fucker.

~*~

Griff looked at the table from every angle and still couldn't decide if he wanted it. The auction that he and Lilac had decided to come to was huge, and there were several pieces that he wanted to get, but this table, it seemed to call to him. He looked at Lilac when she joined him under the tent.

"That's nice." He nodded and told her what he was thinking. "You don't know if it'll fit in your dining room? I would have thought you might have measured that before coming here. What could it hurt if it's too big or small? I'm not trying to bust your balls about this, but really, what would you do if it wasn't the size you wanted?"

"Give it to one of my friends. Or just put it in the barn with a lot of other pieces that Elissa put in there." He grinned at her when she tsked at him. "It would help me a great deal if you could tell me if you like this table or not. I want the dining room to be a special place in our home and your input would help me a great deal."

"You're nuts." She walked around the table as he had, looking under it, lifting it with one or both hands. He figured she was trying to see if she could lift it to help take it in the house, but when she turned to him, he knew that she'd had other reasons. "The foundation of the table is sound. It doesn't shimmy when you move it. Also, it's made of oak that can be refinished if you're into that. I do love to work on wood, but that would be up to you. The chairs that are in the other tent go with it, I think. There are ten of them, and two armchairs that have seen better days. Repairable though. I'd pay no more than a hundred and fifty for this table, less if you could. And not more than about ten apiece on the chairs, as they need more work."

"All right. That's very helpful. And I would like to refinish it with you too. I think that it'll be a lot of work, but well worth it." She nodded and looked at the other pieces that were under the big tent. "Do you see anything else here that goes with the

43

set? I'd like to get it all if I can."

"There is a sideboard in the same tent with the chairs. It too needs some work, but again, that wouldn't be too difficult." She kept looking at the rocker but didn't say anything about it. "There are some extras that you have room for. The hall tree over there. While it doesn't match anything you have, it would matter little if you put it in your front hall."

"I like that idea. There isn't a closet there, so this might be nicer. And it has an umbrella rack on it as well. I like that." She told him of the antique umbrellas that were up for bidding soon, and the two of them made their way there. "I tell you what—since we know what pieces we want, we'll split up. Usually when there are two rings going, I miss out on some of the things I want. You bid on the chairs and the other things in that tent, I'll work this end."

"All right. But the umbrellas, are you wanting them as well? I've looked them over and they're in good shape. Even the carved handles on some of them are in excellent shape, considering how old they appear to be." They were just going under the tent when the umbrellas were held up to be bid on. "I'd not go over much more than about five each for them. They're nice, but not practical."

When no one bid on the umbrellas as choice, the auctioneer said that they could bundle them. When they got down to a dollar, having started out at fifty, he lifted his hand. The man said they were sold quickly, and he got ten of them for one dollar. Griff hadn't had this much fun in a very long time.

When they split up, Lilac staying in the tent with the chairs, he went to the area with the table and rocker. Griff decided that since he'd gotten such a good deal on the other items that she wanted, he'd get her the rocker. Laughing to himself, he knew that he was going to get her the rocker anyway, but this would

44

be his excuse if she fussed at him.

He got the table for twenty-five dollars and the rocker for ten. Things were going his way, so he bid on the two benches that he wanted to put on the deck and got them for a song as well. When the tent he was under was finished up, in addition to the items that he'd bid on first, he'd gotten three boxes of junk when they were thrown in with the benches. Griff went to find Lilac.

She was smiling when he put his arm around her waist. Lilac told him she was doing well, but saw that there was a box of china that she thought would go in the hutch that she'd found. He was glad for the large dining room now, as they had a table, twelve chairs, a credenza, as well as a china hutch. When the dishes came up, Griff fell in love with them. They had a beautiful forest on each of the dinner plates as well as the mugs, and flowers of the forest on the salad plates and other items. He watched as she bid on those.

He could feel her disappointment when the dishware went higher than she wanted to pay. Griff didn't care how much they cost now, he didn't want her to be disappointed. So, he bid on the boxes of them. Griff didn't think that paying twenty-four dollars for what they thought was twelve place settings was a bad deal. But she fussed at him, just as he'd hoped that she would.

"You paid too much for them. I mean, for all you know there might be lots of pieces missing from it. Or all the ones on the bottom of the box broken into small pieces." Griff kissed her quickly on the mouth as he made his way to the boxes. When he carefully set the three of them on his new table, he started taking them out of the box to see. "Oh my, Griff, they're more beautiful than I thought they were."

"Yes. And look, love. We have fourteen place settings, and

45

all of the pieces are here for the hostess set as well. Look at this." He held up the platter that had the same entire scene that was on the plates. "It looks like it could be the woods behind our house. And the colors on this are outstanding."

They held hands as they went around the rest of the auction. The pack had come with them to this to help load up what they purchased. And when they were looking at the box lots, Griff was ready to call it a day when she squealed. Going to her to see what she'd found, Lilac told him to look at the box by her foot.

There were three boxes filled with glassware — stemmed glasses, water and juice ones as well. And they all had etchings on them that looked like they went with the dinnerware set that they'd purchased. She stood guard over the boxes, which he thought was funny as no one seemed to be interested in them, while he went to get them both something to eat. As he was standing in line, Danburn reached out to him.

Do you know a woman by the name of Nancy Shipley? He said that it didn't ring a bell but asked him why. *Two days ago, she took an advertisement out in a lot of newspapers. Kendrick and Cassie were packing some of the things that were in one of the buildings that we purchased. They were using newspaper to pack away some of the glass pieces when they saw your name in the ad. I called the paper, and they directed me to the person in charge of such things. I've got a call out to the woman who put it in, but no word just yet. I thought, while I was waiting, I'd ask you about it.*

What does it say? I mean, is it someone that is looking for me specifically, or just an ad that says she's looking for me? Danburn said that he'd read it to him, to hold on. Griff told Lilac what Danburn was saying when he got back to her with a hotdog and bottles of water.

Here you go. 'Trying to find Griffith Alexander Farley, the fourth

46

Earl of Alexander's Folly. The Duke of Winebarger and Baron of Windemere Castle.' I thought it was a little too specific to think that it wasn't you. But the rest of it says to contact her, Nancy Shipley, as soon as possible. Then there is a post office box number to contact her to find out where to meet her. Griff said that he didn't know who she was. *I didn't remember the name either, but Quinn is looking into it. She can find just about anything when she sets her mind to it.*

All right. Let me know when you find out something. I'm going to take Lilac out to dinner as we've had a wonderful afternoon buying stuff, and we should be home late. If you need me, we're not that far away to come home. Danburn said that they were looking now, but he didn't expect anything to come of it tonight, and to have a good time. *I am. Any word on my brother? Is he causing trouble? I heard what happened at the clinic. I did break his hand badly, but I'm not concerned about it. He was going to hit Lilac.*

You won't hear me complaining about him having a little extra pain. They both laughed. *I'll let you know what I find out; you have fun.*

No one wanted to bid on the boxes up to the ones that they wanted. The auctioneer kept adding the next box and the next until he got to the glasses. There were only a handful of people in the area, but Griff figured, like Lilac did, that they were all waiting on the glasses. When the guy asked for a starting bid, he put up one finger, meaning to ask about how low they could go, when the man smiled at him and said that they were his. For a buck they ended up with fourteen boxes of junk, not including the glassware. He was so excited that he'd won that he picked Lilac up and swung her around.

They were finished then. There were more boxes, but they had what they wanted. Having the pack there to help them carry their load to the table again, they sorted through it all there. In addition to the stemware, they also ended up with a

47

couple of pocket watches, some odds and ends of stationery, as well as two heavy boxes of books. All of that their purchases were loaded into the trailer that they'd rented for the pack to drive home.

"How about some dinner with me? We had a wonderful day, my dear, and I find that I just don't want it to end just yet. There is a nice steakhouse right up the road." She said she was game but wanted to wash her hands and face. "Yes, I did notice that you pick up a lot of dust and grime at these things. We'll have dinner after we clean up, then go on home. It's still early enough that I think we can beat the dinner crowd, don't you think?"

"Yes. And it was a wonderful day, wasn't it? I don't think I've had that much fun at an auction in a good long time." She had a big grin on her face, and he kissed the back of her hand as they made their way back to his truck. "I can't believe that we got everything we wanted, and at a fantastic price too. I'm so excited to see the dishes in the hutch, aren't you?"

"Yes. I'm excited to see it all, as a matter of fact. A couple more auctions like this one and we should have the entire house outfitted. Beds for the spare bedrooms, a few dressers to go with them, and some pieces to put around as accent pieces. You have excellent taste, my dear mate. I love you." He wasn't sure how she'd react to him saying that, so held his breath as they got into the truck. When he helped her in and got in on the other side, she turned and looked at him. "Are you all right?"

"Yes. I was just thinking about how much fun I had, and that I love you as well. I know that you and I have a lot of things to work out, but today was just what I needed to show me that you are nothing like your brother. Thank you for that." He asked her for a kiss, to sort of end the day on a perfect note. "Yes, I'd like that too."

Pulling her to him, Griff tried very hard not to take more than she was willing to give him. But the moment that their mouths touched, he knew that it was going to take everything to try and hold back. The moment that she turned on the seat and settled over his lap, Griff nearly came. Christ, he wanted this woman.

Chapter 4

She hadn't meant to sit on his lap. Hadn't meant to even deepen the kiss that he'd given her. But she needed him, needed him to take her in a way that she'd never experienced before.

When he pulled her blouse up, taking her bra with it, she cried out when he took her nipple into his mouth and nibbled on it. He pulled his head away and she kissed him again, tugging at his own clothing as he moved out from under the steering wheel.

"Someone is going to see us." She moaned against his mouth when he said that he didn't care. "But we should, don't you think?"

"Yes." He rolled her to the seat, settling between her legs as he did so. "Hang onto me, love. This is going to be fast." Getting out of the truck, he looked around, and in moments was his beautiful dragon. When he gathered her into his arms, she thought he was marking her in some way.

Lilac didn't know for sure what he'd meant until they were atop a hill covered in vegetation and trees. Before she could ask him where they were, he stripped her clothing off her and

51

stepped back from her. Lilac felt both exposed and sexy at the same time.

"You're more beautiful than I thought." Lilac started to cover herself, feeling out of her element for a moment, when he pulled her hands away from her breasts and touched his finger to her nipple again. "I'm going to eat you. I want to be able to taste your nectar, the way you smell right now. Like you're a ripe peach that is all mine for the taking."

"Please. I need you." He picked her up, his own body naked now, and pressed her against the tree behind her. When he put her down, her knees were trembling so badly that he held her upright for a few seconds. When he dropped down in front of her, his breath heating her up like a roaring fire never had, Griff slid his fingers into her sheath and suckled on her womanhood at the same time. Crying out with her first orgasm, she held him to her as he feasted on her. Griff ate her like she was going to be his only meal for a great long time.

She came so many times that she lost track. All she knew was that they seemed to start and stop so close together that she was sure that she was going to die from them, one right after the other, each one taking a little more of her. Lilac begged him to stop, told him that she could take no more.

"Ah, but you will, my love. For me."

Griff helped her to the grass, which was soft on her back, her body limp with his administrations. And when he licked her from gate to clit this time, she screamed out her release as if it came from the bottom of her feet. Still he didn't stop.

Over and over he made her come, not giving her a chance to breathe or even to gather her wits about her as he gave her pleasure. And when he sat up, his body hard and glistening in the evening light, she watched as he fisted his cock, using the precum at the tip as a lubricant.

"I'm going to try and take you easily, but I don't hold out much hope for that." She laughed; his face was full of pain, yet he spoke like he'd been telling her of the weather. "Tell me, Lilac — tell me that you belong to me and none other. That you are my mate and will be for the rest of our days."

Without any hesitation, Lilac repeated his vows as well as her own. "I belong to you and none other. My heart belongs to you. I will worship you for the rest of my days and forsake all others. You are my mate, my one and only true love, and I will be with you for all eternity." He kissed her then, his hard cock touching off more small climaxes as he brushed it across her clit. "Please, take me, Griffith."

He slammed home — there were no other words for how he took her. And when she cried out with it, the pleasure of it making her dizzy, he pounded her hard, holding her to his body as he made her his. When he threw back his head, his body stiff with his own release, Lilac watched him, marveling that this man was all hers.

When he came a second time, his body seemed to become a part of her, her heart drowning in the love that he was giving her. Lilac rose up, her body bowing up to meet him when she came. Her body flew apart, then slammed back together when he cried out for the third and final time. Darkness didn't just come over her in that moment but seemed to make her entire life blink out. The last thing that she remembered was him falling atop her, and then nothing.

When she woke, Lilac was in the big bed at their home, alone. There was a note beside her on the pillow that had gone cold without him there. Picking it up, she was smiling so much that her face hurt with it.

My darling Lilac. I am deeply in love with you. I have gone to get the truck. The auctioneer wasn't thrilled about us leaving it there. So

53

alas, I had to leave you in our bed to get it. But I will be back soon, hopefully before you get to read this. Then he signed it Griff.

Getting up, she realized that it was much later than she'd thought it was. The sun was up, but thanks to the darkening shades in the room, the sun coming into the room hadn't bothered her. Stretching out some of the kinks from last night, she got up to get a shower.

By the time she got out of the shower, she'd tried to reach Griff several times and was getting worried. Dressing hurriedly, she made her way down the stairs to find that not only wasn't Griff home, but that Kip and Dana were in the kitchen.

"What's happened?" Neither man seemed inclined to talk, so she slammed her hands down on the table and asked again. "Where is he and how do we get him back here?"

"Someone called me when they discovered his truck smashed up against a tree not ten miles from here. We came here first because we wanted to make sure that first of all, he wasn't here, and that you were safe." She asked Dana what they'd been able to find out. "Nothing as yet. The truck has been totaled, and there was a lot of blood, his. But being a dragon, he won't die, and we're hoping that he's just been taken and not wandering around with a head injury right now."

"And how is that supposed to be comforting?" Dana looked at Kip. They were trying their best to break it to her gently, but she wasn't having it. "Tell me, damn it. I need to know so that I can find him."

"We've asked Mother Earth to help in locating him. Nothing so far. So, he's either on some stones or he's up off the ground. But she's looking for him too." Lilac asked what else they were doing. "The entire pack is out looking, as well as most of the townspeople. Rett has called an emergency meeting, and is sending out men in groups all over the grounds. Nothing so far."

Lilac pulled off her shoes as Dana continued to tell her what was going on. The dragons were out looking, as were all the people in the little town they lived in. Lilac asked him about the faeries.

"We have a few that we know, but not well enough to ask them to help us find him. Dana and I were hoping that you being a faerie, you could get them together faster than we could." She reached out for Sunny and told her to come to her. "Also, you should know that we don't think it was his brother. It might well have been, but his scent isn't anywhere near the accident, nor did we find anything around the wreckage that would indicate he was nearby. Someone, however, ran him off the road, and we're looking into that as well. Whoever it was, they weren't human. But for now, that's all I can tell you for sure."

Sunny showed up just as she was thinking what she had to do next. Dana thanked her as she spoke to her faerie helper. She was sick with worry now, and she thought that Sunny could tell.

"He's been missing for some time. I need for you to go to the wreckage and find out what you can. Also, please call on the others and have them search every cave and every tree around here. There is blood at the scene, so that might help you." Sunny said that she had a great army that would also help. "I know, and I thank you for that. Tell them that we'll take any news that they can get back to me. Anything. All right?"

"Yes, my lady." Sunny started away and then returned to sit upon her hand. "The brother, we will have some people look for him as well. I know that you were told that he wasn't nearby, but we'll go to him as well."

Lilac wasn't sure what to do, so she went outside to sit on

the earth. She'd been told that someone had asked the queen of the faeries for help, but as she had a special bond with her that no one knew about, she sat very still when asking—no, pleading for help.

"Hello, my daughter. I have heard a great many things about you." She thanked her and told her of her love. "Yes, I have been searching everywhere that I can for him. Even in caves that have not been visited in decades. Griffith, he is very special to myself as well. And is my son now. Should you like to add your strength to those that are searching for him, I will replenish you quickly."

Lilac reached to the water, all manner of waterways, from the lakes and oceans to the small streams that snaked along the caves that surrounded her. Speaking to the water in ways that few could, she had it seeking every corner, every darkened space—even the rain that tumbled down around the trees so that they were fed. She knew that the water at the falls near the castle keep had stilled to hear her request. The creeks that were there for the creatures to use also stopped moving to listen to what she, the queen of the water, had to say.

My mate is missing. Griffith is a great dragon, a man that I love. He may be injured and not able to tell us where he is. I beg of you, waterways of my kind, please search the stones that you are a part of, the lakes that are nearby. I need to find my other half and see to his needs. They answered in kind, telling her that they'd seek everywhere they flowed, would use all of their resources to find her king. *I thank you. I will come to you soon, all of you, to replenish you for this help you have given me.*

Nay, our daughter. There is no need for that. The king of dragons, he has given us more than we could ever hope to use. We are bountiful in our fishes. Our waters are clear of anything that would harm us. The animals that sip from us, they are well because we are. Lilac

56

thanked them again. *It is we that thank you, my lady queen. To ask such a thing of us, we are honored to serve you.*

She was ready to leave this area and go to the place where the accident occurred when she heard from the waterways in the mountain. He told her that the stones that protected him had found a man such as the one she spoke of.

I will guide you to him, my lady. Listen to the water as you get closer to the mountain cave that can be seen from the crushed metal. She asked if he was injured. *Yes, my lady, but not as badly as I first thought. He is healing, but laying still upon a warmed stone.*

Telling the others where she was going, all of them told her that they'd meet her there. The ones from the house spilled out into the yard, shifting into their dragons to move quickly to the spot.

Spreading out her wings, she knew what she must look like to them and decided to tell them later. She was going to find Griff, and there wasn't time to explain why she was so different than all the other faeries that were making this place their home. Taking to the skies, she had to follow them because she'd not heard where the accident had occurred. As soon as she saw the truck, her heart seemed to stop beating for a second or two.

The pretty blue truck was smashed against a large tree. Then entire top of it, the roof, was torn away from the body of it, like a large can opener had been used. The glass was, of course, broken out of the front, as well as on the driver's side. The back end, the bed, was filled with broken glass and trees, even a few stones. Some of the tires had gone flat.

Lilac landed next to the tree and gave it a little of herself to heal it as well.

The mountain in front of you, where the cherries bloom every spring and the trees are golden in the fall. You will see it, my lady, if you look for an opening in the great belly of the earth. Lilac repeated what was being said to her and Hanson found it immediately. *He is deep within the belly, my lady, resting now and awaiting you to come for him.*

You have spoken to him? He told her that he had, that he was as she was, their king to her queen. *I've not told him as yet what I am. Have you?*

He knows now.

Lilac wondered how he'd react to that news, but so long as he was safe, she didn't care if Griff was angry with her for not telling him. The waters spoke to her all the way to the cave and beyond.

When she found her love, he was sitting next to a stone warmed by his breath as his dragon. Lilac ran the last few feet to him and leaned into his large body. He patted her gently, his large claws bigger than she was. And when she looked up at him, Lilac could see that he was upset, but decided that this was a conversation for later. Not in a deep cave where their voices would echo, and all would know what they said.

~*~

Griff was helped from the cave by Dana and Danburn. He had yet to tell them what had happened. Telling them would make it so real, and he wasn't sure that he could handle that for now. Instead, he focused on what the water had said to him. Water that he'd never been able to converse with before. He was a king.

While he could understand why she'd not told him what she was, it still hurt him that she would keep something so big from him. A queen—his mate was the queen of the water, and he hadn't any idea until then. Griff said that he was all right now, and sat upon the large stone that was just outside his hiding place.

"You really scared us, Griff." Danburn sat on another stone

58

and shook his head as he continued. "Had it not been for Lilac, I'm not sure how much longer you would have been there. Why didn't you call out when you woke?"

"I wasn't sure who would be able to hear me." He looked at Lilac, who was now sitting quietly as far from him as she could get. "I have to tell you what happened. I need to, but it boggles my mind to tell you that it was my mother who ran me off the road. She sat in the middle of the road as I was driving and swiped her hand to the front of the truck, knocking me to the ditch when I tried to avoid her."

He watched Lilac. She'd had nothing to do with this, but he still was upset with her. To keep such a thing from him was just the same as lying. They had only just discussed this very thing. And now he'd found out that not only was she the queen of the waters, but she was daughter to the queen of faeries as well.

"We'll get you home now, and figure this out later. I have to look into a few things as well. If your mother is around here and causing trouble, then I will need to find her for several more reasons than just trying to kill my good friend." Danburn asked him if he could fly. "If not, one of us can carry you. You've given us all enough to be worried about, so if you can't, then we'd gladly take you home."

He said that he could fly and asked that they all just let him rest. They'd do that for him, he knew that, but his real reason was that he wanted to talk to Lilac. Griff was hoping that she could tell him why she'd do such a thing.

As soon as the rest of them were gone, having asked him several times if he was all right, he turned and looked at Lilac. "You didn't tell me what you were. Telling us, in fact, that you were nothing more than a faerie. Why would you do that?" She got up off the stone and started to pace. He let her, knowing that rushing her would get him nothing.

"I didn't trust you." He knew that, but had hoped they were past that by now, and said that to her. "Yes, I do trust you, but we only got to that point yesterday. And while I could have told you before, I was terrified that your brother would find out. And should he do that, then we'd never have peace from him."

"I understand." He did, too. And she was correct in them only just trusting each other with their feelings. "The water that spoke to me, it said that you were also the daughter to the queen of the faeries. That you are the queen of all the waters. Keeping that from me, while I do understand, you can imagine my pain when I had to find out from the water speaking to me."

"I am sorry about that. I don't know that I had plans to tell you. It was something that I have been holding to my chest for many years. To be caught, to be held by someone, was a greater possibility if someone knew. If I am captured and this person would know about my status, they could in turn order me to do great harm to the earth with my contact with the waters." He asked her what that meant. "Unlike you, a creature that has his own mind and is able to decide what he'd like to do or not, I must do whatever is told to me if I'm caught. Much like a faerie. I am not a master of myself. Not until someone claims me as such."

"You mean that had James known what you were, he could have commanded you to destroy the lands with your water?" She said that there was more to it than that. "Such as? Again, I'm not sure why I wasn't made aware of this."

"You and your brother are twins. Did you know that he can read your mind because he is the elder of the two of you?" Griff said that he knew, but hadn't thought about it in some time. "You can block him out now, being a dragon of worth. But should he want, he could breach your mind and find out

60

all manner of things simply because you didn't think about keeping him out, am I correct? He would know that you have a vault of gems at your disposal. You have money that isn't in the banks. If he were to capture me, as he had, and know what I was, then I could not have come to you as your mate. He could have controlled that, because he would have claimed me and my talent."

Griff tried to run this through his mind. There were so many questions that he had, but he thought that if he gave himself a moment, he'd get it. Just sitting there, his mind working out what she'd said to him, something else occurred to him. Griff looked at Lilac.

"He thinks my mother is dead. I thought that he and she had gotten together to end my life. But it's not that, is it? Why would she try and harm me, do you know?" Lilac told him that she didn't but had a theory. "What is it? Right now, I can't think beyond my mother being alive and then knocking me into a ditch."

"She may have thought you were your brother." He'd not thought of that and told her. "You said that James killed your father, that he removed his head. Is this something that your mom would have known? I mean, before she was being fed the iron?"

"Yes, it wasn't until several weeks later — I would say about five — that she became ill and took to her bed. But feeding her iron the way that I think he was, I was always confused as to how that might have killed her." Lilac said that she'd bet she knew what he was doing. "You think that she might have faked her illness or how bad it was so that she could get away?"

"I do. And if he would do such a thing to his parents, what do you think he would have done with me should he have known?" Griff said that he would have destroyed her. "Yes,

61

and anything that we hold dear on this earth. I would have had little to no choice but to do his bidding."

"And now—do you have to listen to him now if he were to capture you?" She said that so long as Griff didn't claim her, she was fair game, even if they were mated. "Then how do I claim you? Because as much as I love you, I don't want him to get you that much more."

"You have to ask my mother for me. To claim me from her." Griff nodded, thinking that it had to be much harder than it sounded. "You have to call to her, as you don't have me shackled to you. Then you ask her, not just her but all the creatures of the earth, if you might claim me as your own."

"When can I do that? Now would suit me just fine." She laughed and Griff smiled. To hear her laughing when they were being so serious did great things to his heart. "I love you, my dearest Queen Lilac."

"Hello, my son and my daughter." Griff stood up and bowed low to the woman who made her appearance before him. She was much too bright for him to look at. Her crown and wings were brilliant in the waning evening. "Please, we're family now, and I'd like nothing better than to help the man who has stolen the heart of my child."

"I have a wish to claim her as my own, my lady. She has only just told me what I must do or I would have done it much sooner." Griff took Lilac's hand in his when she reached out to him. "She is my mate, the other half of me that keeps me alive. I want to claim her for that reason, but not that one alone. I love her, with all that I have. My dragon is in love with her as well. We wish to keep her safe. To keep her with us for all time."

"You do this willingly, my son, Griffith of the dragons, king to the water? You will take her hand in yours from this day forward?" Griffith said that he would, easily. "And your wish to claim her, as she is, the queen to the water? You will keep her safe above all others, and never stray from her side?"

"Nay, my lady, I will never leave her side, and I accept being king to her queen."

He looked at the ground when it rumbled beneath his feet. Bending over, he unearthed a gem, one made of the most beautiful emerald he'd ever seen. When he pulled it from the warm earth, he realized that it was a ring; a better one he could not have wished for.

"You will need to put the ring to her heart first, to claim that part of her." He did this, and to the rest of her body as he was directed. "To her belly so that children will grow there, safely nestled within her. To her arms, so that she will have strength to be strong enough to keep you safe as well. And lastly to her eyes, so that she can only see you and how much that you cherish and love her. Please put the ring upon her finger, Griffith, king of the waters."

Slipping the ring onto her finger, he had a moment of worry when it was much too large for her delicate hand. But almost as soon as he thought that, the ring adjusted itself to fit her, even making the stone smaller for her tiny hands. Kissing first her hand that held his promise, he kissed her as well. She was his, in all ways, and he was hers. They looked at his new mother-in-law and smiled at her.

"I cannot thank you enough for this, my lady. To have her in my life—she's more than I could have ever hoped for in a mate." The queen nodded and told him to call her by her name, Kassina. "Thank you, Lady Kassina."

The two of them made their way back to the house, walking slowly, stopping to smell the fresh flowers, to marvel at the intricate spider webs that were still covered in a fine dew. They spoke little, the two of them. But Griff didn't mind. Lilac was his mate, and to him there weren't words enough to tell anyone how that made him feel.

Chapter 5

James moved around the hotel rooms that he'd taken for himself and tried to think what had happened that woke him in such a state. Even before the sun had risen, he'd sort of gone from a rested state to full out horrific terror in a matter of seconds. He'd been so terrified that his body was drenched in sweat. And he had been trembling so hard that he'd bitten his lip and hurt his teeth. But the good news was, his hand was mostly healed, and he could at least bend his fingers without being ill.

He couldn't remember having any dreams. There weren't any monsters chasing after him that he could remember. Even the room, for as hot as it had been during the day, was cooled off enough that the feeling of being burned alive seemed stupid now. But something had awakened him, and he'd been afraid to close his eyes afterwards.

"What if someone came into my place to hurt me? What other reason could I have to have woke like that?" He'd always spoken to himself. His thinking was that no one else could give him the best answers. James knew that some would think him mad, but he was far from that. James knew himself to be extremely smart. It was just that people didn't listen to him when he spoke, so they did not understand him fully.

He went back out to the car. It looked all right. There were no marks on it to indicate that someone had tampered with it. James was glad now that he'd not had it washed when he'd last filled up. This way the fingerprints were right there for him to see should he be messed with.

Eating his small meal of packaged noodles, he wondered what his woman was doing now. She'd be bringing him a nice meal, with all the things that he liked. Of course, that didn't mean that he'd let her be unchained. Nor did he think that she'd not poison him. No, a person like her would run again or try to kill him. James wondered, still, who had unchained her while he'd been away.

"It had to be Griffith. He was always jealous of me." That wasn't true either, he told himself. He'd been the one that had always been jealous of his younger brother. "He has it all, while I'm left with nothing. It's unfair that I was not the one that received all the riches of being born to a dragon. And here he is flaunting it around like he's something special. Mother should have taken better care that I was the one to be the dragon."

He thought that was why he'd taken such pleasure in killing his parents. They both should have suffered more than they had, to his way of thinking. Even his father, down on his knees before him, didn't beg for his life when he told him—a lie, yes—that he'd allow him to go if he should beg him. He only stared at him with those green eyes that James had not gotten either. They were for Griffith too.

"Why did no one think that I'd be so looked over when I was born? And who allowed me to be born with a brother anyway? I should have been the only one that was born. Did anyone think it strange or even wrong that I got nothing from my parents?" James went back into his hovel, the place that was looking more and more like the castle had before his brother took that from him as well. "The mother fucker just had to rub it into my face that he now owns what rightfully should be mine. The very least he could have done was tell me that he'd allow me to live in it. It was mine, according to the laws of our kind."

What kind was he? James wondered. He wasn't a dragon — didn't even have dragon strength. He wasn't human either. Being an immortal told him that much. He could also heal faster, but not as quickly as Griffith could. And he was stronger than the average human, as well as the ability to read minds, so long as they were close enough for him to touch at the time.

"Griffith, the fucker, can probably do all that and more without having to have limitations on how he can do it." Making his dinner was easy, especially since he had no water or stove, and certainly no way to have the trash picked up after him if he were to toss it across the room as he had last evening. "I bet he has a houseful of servants. And they wipe his ass for him when he takes a shit, too."

Laughing while he complained made him feel better. He knew that there were servants at his brother's home. Hell, he'd had them too when there was money to pay them. But one day, he woke up and not only were they gone, but they'd taken some things from him to compensate for the salary he'd not given them in months.

Then Griffith took his home, the family home, right out from under him. That was still burning his ass, the way that he'd had the money to pay off the back taxes and the liens against the place, and to have it cleaned up. The lawns, what used to be his father's pride and joy, had been in ruin — most of the bushes that surrounded the house were dead. The trees, once a source of fruit for the castle, had died from lack of care. Now all that was viable again. The lawns looked as good if not better than when his father had been alive. Even the fruit in the trees was plentiful, their bounty endless, it seemed to James. Yet none of it was his to use.

The gardens, herb as well as vegetable, had been so overgrown when he'd been there that it was difficult to tell where the gardens started and the grass ended. And only when the yard had been mowed, which wasn't often, could you tell that there had been something wonderful there. The smell of the vegetation that was struggling to push through would scent the air for hours afterwards.

But without cooks, why bother with an herb garden? The same with the yard. James thought it had been at least a decade since he'd bothered with having the lawn mowed or the trees trimmed. Why bother? It wasn't as if anyone would visit him. Not when they could hang around with his asshole brother.

"And now look at how far I've fallen. I've nothing, not a single piece of the jewelry that Mother left behind when I killed her. Not one pipe that Father used to smoke in the evenings. All of it gone. Gone to the pawn shops and other places that would take his things for cash. I hope that my selling off the family things has bothered Griffith very badly."

Toward the end of his staying at the house, there had been few pickings left anyway. He'd lost a great deal of it while playing poker with his buddies and having lavish meals when he should have been saving. But he'd been the king of the castle, the oldest son of the lord and lady of his home. He wasn't sure how he'd lost so much in such a short amount of time, but he knew that he'd had a great deal of fun while he'd been at it.

Griffith had always had it all. Women galore, nice clothing that he would hang up in his closet and keep nice. James had known there were servants to clean up after him, and made them earn their keep. But not his brother. Griffith even had his first car still. The one that had been purchased by him when he'd gotten out of college, again, just recently.

Waste not, want not was something that had been drilled into their heads since infancy. James hadn't heeded that saying, spending when he had it, ruining more than he should have, and never setting foot in any school rooms beyond what was required of him by law.

After he finished off his dry noodles, he got into his car and made his way into town. He was getting good at stealing what he needed from the local idiots. But today he was going to get something that he could heat up a meal in. He had no idea how he was going to make that work—there wasn't any electricity at the hotel. But by God, he was sick of eating food from a can, and noodles that were much too crunchy for his tastes.

There were any number of stores that he could have hit up for food, and clothing, for that matter. If he wanted to look cheap, that was. While he knew the value of money, it was only when he didn't have any that he wanted to spend more of it. It was really fucked up, thinking that way, but he wasn't known for his fashion sense for nothing.

Moving in and out of aisles, he picked the things he was going to take. There was a great deal today too, as they were not only getting a large delivery of canned goods, but there was also a truck that had milk and eggs in it, as well as one that had some lunchmeat, bacon, and hams. He decided to try and swipe the things even before they got on the shelves. But once outside, he realized that wasn't going to work at all.

There were two cops parked in the lot. They didn't seem to be paying any attention to him or what was going on around them. But he knew better than to think just because they looked uninterested, they'd not be all over him if he tried something. So, as he walked by the large truck that was full of meats, he only took what he could carry under his shirt and left what he really wanted. Bacon.

Tossing what he'd gotten to the back seat of his car, he covered what he'd gotten with his old jacket and hoped that it'd not get too warm while he finished up today. Going into a second store, he was able to get him a few other items, as well as a hot plate.

That had been the hardest thing to get out of the store. He had nearly gotten caught twice with it when he'd been trying to get it under his shirt. Then as he was going out the door at the same time as another person, the doors had made a godawful racket that made him think that he'd surely been caught. But it hadn't been for him. The person that had been about to go out with him went back to the register, saying that he didn't know what was going on. James escaped with his hot plate, as well as enough food for a few more days. Now he had to figure out how to use it.

The next place that he'd hit was much easier than the first two. He was able to snag him some underwear, shampoo, as well as a few towels and some bar soap. James would have much preferred some of the soft soap that came in the most delicious flavors, but he wasn't able to stand there and sniff each one to figure out what he wanted. That he blamed on his brother as well.

By the time he was headed back to the hotel, he was feeling pretty damn good about his things. He had food now, a way to cook it—when he figured that out—as well as some much-needed clean clothing. And a way to clean himself up.

As soon as he pulled into the lot, however, he could only sit in his car and watch. The place had caught fire. Not only that,

70

but the thing looked as if it had been burning for some time. The fire department was hosing down the roof, which he didn't understand. It looked to him like it was a total loss. There were police there too, moving traffic around so that no one could get close enough to get burned.

"Well, mother fuck." James got out of his car to watch the only home he had right now go down in a ball of flames, along with the things that he'd stashed in there—a few changes of clothing, a case of water that he'd stolen. There had been other things too. Nothing of worth, not really, but they'd been his.

"This is all his fault. Griffith did this. How else would a perfectly good place go up in flames like this? It's not as if there had been anything running—there wasn't any fucking power to the place." James was going to have to start keeping track of all the things that Griffith had done to him.

He was startled out of his thinking when a police officer asked him if he knew anyone that might have been staying there.

"No, I can't say that I do. I only stopped to see what all the commotion is about. Do you know who did it?" The officer said they didn't think it was arson, if that was what he'd been asking. "I wasn't, but I didn't think this place had any power to it. What would have made it go off like this?"

"We think it was just old and ready to go anyway. The fire department thinks it might have been smoldering for some time, perhaps since the last storm we had rolling through here. Lightning might have hit it, and nobody noticed it until it was out of hand." James only nodded. He knew who had done it and why. "There was a squatter living in the place, but we don't believe they had anything to do with the fire. Homeless people are fairly good about not setting fire to some place that they live."

71

"I'm not homeless. I have a perfectly good home that my brother took from me." The officer looked at him oddly, and James tried to cover up his blunder. "What I mean is, I can't believe that there are homeless people around here. I myself have a home, and wondered why everyone doesn't."

If the officer believed him, he didn't have any idea. About the time he was opening his mouth to say something back to him, someone called the officer away. James got into his car and drove off before he got himself into more trouble. But where to go, that was the fifty-four-thousand-dollar question.

Now he had to find him a place to live and store his newly acquired shit. He'd prefer one that had some hot water and a way to use his hotplate. He had gone to a great deal of trouble to get himself one. But there were few places around that he could move into, other than being in the downtown area. By nightfall, however, he was getting desperate, and made himself at home in one of the four buildings in the downtown area that wasn't being worked on.

"This is bullshit. Why am I having to lower myself to living in a decrepit place when I have a castle that is mine?" James had no answer to his question, but he did stew on it for the rest of the evening. "Hopefully something will befall my brother, and I'll not have to put up with him again. That's just what I need. Him gone."

~*~

Danburn loved having his family here. His mom had requested that they all get together for dinner, and it wasn't any trouble getting his fellow dragons to come as well. She loved these men as much if not more than he did. They'd been friends longer than most people lived. And he could not have asked for better ones.

"I should like to make a toast." His mother pinged her knife to her wine glass and everyone turned to her. "I would like to thank each and every one of you for coming here this evening. I want to tell you, from the bottom of my heart, how much you have all have come to mean to me over the decades. Some of you less time than that, but no less in my heart."

"Danburn, it's time." He nodded to Kendrick's whisper as his mother continued thanking everyone for being there. "Danburn, I'm not joking."

"I know, honey, but dinner will be served soon and we'll— What did you say?" She told him again that it was time. "Time? You mean, it's time time?"

"I haven't any idea what that means, but if you mean the baby, then yes, you moron, it's time for that." He leapt from his chair and ran out of the dining room. Kendrick was laughing when she called him back. "Danburn? Did you forget something?"

"No." He came back when he realized that he'd forgotten his wife. When everyone at the table stood up too, he got the pleasure of seeing each of their faces, including his mom's, when he made the announcement. "Kendrick says that it's time. I'm going to be a father."

He fell to the floor then, everything that he'd been looking forward to over the last months hitting him right between the eyes. He was going to be a father. Danburn looked up at the face in front of him—it just happened to be his mother's.

"Son are you all right?" He nodded, then shook his head. "Yes, well, I can see that. It's all so perfectly clear to us all. Are you going to sit on your bottom here in the dining room, or go up to your room to help your wife bring your child into the world?"

"I'm not ready, Mom." She laughed at him and he felt like an idiot. "I'm going to mess this up. Perhaps it's a false alarm and we have a bit more time? Please?"

About the time he was finished speaking, he felt her pain like it was his own. Kendrick was in labor. She was going to bring his child into the world whether he was ready or not. He stood up and made his way up the stairs slowly. Danburn needed time, and thought that if he wasn't in the room with her, then she'd not be able to have the child. Christ, he was losing it.

When he entered the room where she was, he looked at his wife. Even working as hard as she was, she still looked beautiful. Going to the side of the bed while the other women prepared her for the baby, Danburn held her hand and told her how much he loved her.

"I love you too. I'm glad that you decided to join us." Her temper was high, and he tried his best not to argue with her right now. He would normally have argued back, loving the way her face turned red and she didn't hold back when she was pissed at him. "Where the fuck are my pain meds? They promised me something for pain. I'd better fucking have something for pain, Danburn, or so help me, you're going to feel every pain that I do."

He believed her. The way she was gripping his hand made him glad that his cock was out of her reach. He had a feeling she'd be holding it hostage instead until this was over. And maybe well beyond that. Kissing the back of her hand again, he told her how much he loved her.

"Danburn, I don't know if you've noticed this or not, but this isn't the time for you to be romantic. I'm in labor, for Christ's sake." Everyone in the room laughed, including his mom. When the next contraction gripped her, she screamed out her agony and squeezed his hand harder than he thought possible for someone of her size. The midwife finally showed up when he thought that his fingers would never be the same again.

The labor seemed to go on forever. It had only been a couple of hours, but to him it felt as if it had been several lifetimes. He didn't want her in pain, and he didn't want her to be pissy with him. But when the midwife told him it was time, he held onto Kendrick's hand. She pushed their child out of her body and into the hands of the woman there. Just like that, he'd gone from being just a man to being someone's dad.

"It's a girl, my lord. And she looks of her mother." He held Kendrick's hand as the child was laid on her chest. She was screaming at the top of her little lungs then, and he touched his finger to the tiny fingers that she was fluttering around like she wanted to slug someone. "She is as beautiful as her mother, I think."

Kendrick cried and laughed when she held their child. And when asked if she wanted to nurse her, they both said that they did, as if he had any say over her doing this. When his daughter latched onto her mother to nurse, Danburn thought it to be the most beautiful sight that he'd ever witnessed. And it would probably be for the rest of his days, too.

He held them both while the bed was cleaned up. Holding his girls was something that, before Kendrick, he'd never thought he'd enjoy. Watching them both as they dozed in his arms, he lifted them up and put them to bed when they said it was ready. Danburn wanted to lie down with them, hold them both forever. But there were others that needed to know that he was a father, so after kissing them both, he made his way to his friends.

"It's a girl. Healthy and happy, she has all her fingers and toes as well as the cutest little button nose I've ever seen." His friends all hugged him, telling him congratulations. "Kendrick is doing well too. They're both sleeping after all their hard work. And Mother is over the moon in love with her already."

"As are you, old man." He nodded and told Rett that he was. "Good, that's the way that it should be. I'm very happy for you both. I've been asked, when the child was born, to declare it a holiday. I think that's a brilliant idea, and will work on a celebration to commemorate her birth as the princess of dragons."

The midwife joined them in the hallway and told them that she was healthy and happy, weighing in at just over eight pounds and a good twenty-three inches long. She also commented on how well Lady Kendrick was doing, and that they were both sleeping soundly.

Next he had to make an announcement to the town. It had been set up weeks ago when the town had hired a town crier for this event. Calling the man up who had been assigned the job, he told him all that he could and said that she'd be named later, when his wife was rested. After hanging up, he looked at Griffith as he joined him in the office.

"You're a very lucky dragon, I think." Danburn said that he felt like he was too. "I'm very proud to be your friend, Danburn, and that I was able to be here when you had your first of what I'm assuming will be many children."

"Yes. I don't know how she feels about having more right at this moment, but we have talked about having a great many children." He laughed with his friend, then looked at him. "What is it, my man? Whatever it is, we can fix it. The way that I'm feeling at this moment, I could fix anything and feel very good about it. Tell me so that we can celebrate as only dragons can."

"My mother is alive." Whatever he expected him to say, that wasn't it. He knew that Griff had said that she'd knocked him off the road, but he thought it was just his head injuries talking. He asked him how sure he was. "Very much so. And in order to explain to you how I'm so sure, I have to tell you that Lilac is the queen of the waterways. Her mother is none other than the queen of the faeries."

"Holy shit." Griff nodded and sat down in the chair across from the desk and him. "When did you find that out? I'm assuming recently."

"When I was found in the cave. She told me, and I know this is true, that she didn't trust me enough to let me know that. She was terrified that James would have claimed her. Claimed her in the way of what she is." Danburn said that it was a ritual that had to be said. "Yes. That's it. And when I said the vow to her mother and her, I was able to receive all that she is. And her me, but for the shifting to dragon."

"She's going to be hunted if anyone finds out. Just knowing that she's a water faerie would have people coming after her, but this—this is something that she won't be able to hide for long." Griff told him of his plan and what he'd done to start on this. "That's a big undertaking, even for you. How do you propose to keep you both hidden away with your brother out there?"

"I've already made arrangements. There is enough magic surrounding all our homes that I don't have to worry about James getting in. The lands and the homes have been fortified so that no one will enter unless we say so." Danburn asked him about his mother. "I don't know what to think about that, to be honest with you. If she's alive and hiding out, I can well understand why. But to not have any contact with me, even after all this time, I find that strange, don't you?"

"Yes. Unless she might not know how to tell who is who between you and James. I have to admit, there were times when you were younger that even I had some trouble with that." Griff said he'd thought of that as well. "And what did you come up with?"

"That I'm going to reach out to her, just to find out what her thinking is. I've no reason to believe that she'd be against me in any way. But I just don't know. And I'm not sure how I feel about her just coming around in time to try and kill me. Had I not ducked when I did, my head would have been removed when her claw took the roof off my truck." Danburn had noticed that as well, but hadn't mentioned it to anyone in the event that he was too stressed and making too much of what he'd thought he had seen. "Kassina said that she'd be able to find her better than we would. So, I have asked her to find out what she could. Just as you were telling us about your daughter, she got back to me to tell me that my mother is staying in the mountains not far from the castle keep. She can't enter either, though I don't know if she has tried."

"Will you let me go with you?" Griff said that he had hoped that he would ask. "As soon as I have things settled here, we'll go. I know that Kendrick is in good hands, and she'll more than likely want to go. Keeping her here to rest might be harder than it will be to confront your mother."

They both laughed and Griff stood when he did. "I'm sorry to have brought this to you today of all days. I didn't know who else to talk to about it. Lilac wants me to call her out, just have a showdown, but I'm hoping that it won't come to that. But again, I just don't know."

"I understand both of your wants in this. I don't know how I would feel either, to be honest. My mother would have stayed, confronted your brother, and ended his miserable life. But your mother was so timid, so unlike my own." Griff laughed, telling him that was an understatement. "Yes, I'm glad that you agree. I'll talk to Kendrick and get back to you. I think that we should try and do this as soon as we can. There is no reason to put off the meeting. Don't you agree?"

"Yes. Thank you, Danburn. And if this turns out to be something nefarious, then you'll be there to help me through it as well." Danburn asked what Lilac's thoughts about this were, to meet up with his mom. "She'd like to take her on, as I said, but since she was the first person to point out she might not know the differences between James and I, she's willing, for now, to give her the benefit of the doubt on this. I hope that she's right, but a large part of me thinks that this is so wrong."

Danburn did as well but didn't voice his concerns to Griff. He had enough going on in his mind for him to be adding to it. Making his way back up to the bedroom where his family was, he watched them both sleep and wondered what sort of life he was going to have now with a little girl in his home. The best, he told himself.

Danburn had it all, as far as he was concerned. A wife that he loved more than life itself. A daughter who already had him wrapped around her little finger. A mother that loved him as much as he did her, and friends that had stood by him at every turn of his life. But Griff — he was worried about Griff and this unknown meeting.

Chapter 6

Marissa wanted to go out and enjoy life again, but she knew that until things were settled around the castle and her sons, she had to stay hidden. She'd already tipped her hand in going after one of them. To do so again would have grave consequences, she thought. It was times like this that she so missed her husband. He would have known just what to do.

Walking back, deeper into the belly of the mountain, she thought about what she'd done. She'd nearly killed one of her children, and it had been the wrong one. Thinking about it now, she knew that she'd have some explaining to do, and only hoped that someone would give her a chance to tell her side of what had happened.

She'd thought it was James, not that it made it all right to have tried to kill him. But James had been the one that had killed her one and only love, and had tried, in vain, to kill her. To think that she'd brought him into the world with such hope, to have had him poison her so heinously. But then, what did she expect to happen when he'd already killed his own father? She missed John more every day.

When she'd discovered that she was being fed iron, her first instinct had been to confront James, to ask him what he was doing. But she thought about how he'd killed his father, and realized that he'd not quit until she too was dead. Faking her illness and then disappearing as she did was the only way that she knew to survive him. And then she'd heard about the castle.

The castle had been in her family for more years, for more generations than she could count now. Her parents had raised her and her brother there, as her mother's parents had raised her. The home had been comfortable, homey, and the heart of their family. But even that stood no chance against James.

He had pilfered all that he could from it, even stripping the tapestries from the walls and selling off heirlooms that could never be replaced. The wild parties that he held, the people coming into her family home, had destroyed even her flower gardens, again something that had been in her family for a long time.

"Oh Griffith, can you ever forgive me?" She mourned the loss of her son. Not that he was dead, but to be able to speak to him. To have him there when she just needed someone to hug her. And when she'd disappeared from his life, she hurt when he'd grieved her passing as if she were dead. Griffith had always held her heart in the same way that James had held her hatred of him.

She thought of the look on Griffith's face when he'd realized it was her trying to kill him that day. By the time she had come to the conclusion that it was Griffith driving the truck, it had been too late for her to bring her anger back. The swipe across his truck, the one that had nearly severed his head, had been meant for James. She would gladly go to the gallows for killing him if it would make her son, her Griffith, safe. James had no love for anyone but himself and money. She'd never raised him to be so selfish, and was always surprised when he showed that side of himself to her. Especially after murdering his own father.

"What have you done, James?" He only shrugged at her, telling her to mind her own business. "But you are covered in blood. Covered in the blood of your sire, your own father. How could you?"

"It was simple, really. I had him down on his knees, and told him just what I was going to do if he didn't leave me the castle now and all the money that went with it. I'm going to get it anyway—I just didn't see any reason for me to wait until he was dead to have it. So I helped him along in that." He looked at her then. "You had best watch your step, Mother dear. I might just find that I have no use for you either. And trust me when I tell you, I'm looking very hard for a way to end your life as well."

It was then that she had someone tell him about iron for a dragon. That to feed it to her, in small doses, would be all it took for him to kill her too. She thought that if he did that to her, fed her iron over a period of a few weeks, she'd be safer than for him to come up with another plan, one that she'd have no control over. And if she was honest with herself, she'd never thought that he'd do it, not try and kill his own mother. But he had. And that was all it took to tip her feelings for her first born to hatred rather than love.

So, on the tenth morning, she had told her trusted advisor what she was going to do, and he was to keep her in the loop of what James did to his brother. Marissa thought that Griffith would have been next on James's list, and that he'd try and kill him as well. But when she'd left him there, the man who had kept her sane during all the happenings of the castle—

her advisor Philip—had been killed along with the rest of the household that had anything to do with her. Her maid, her cook, as well as the milliner that made her gowns for her when she and her husband would travel or have a party—all dead.

She wasn't sure what to do now. Should she find Griffith, tell him what she'd done? Did she send him a message and hope that it would get to him and not his brother? If he should get it over Griffith, what would he do? Marissa knew what he'd do. He'd come for her and end her life just as he had his father's.

Looking at the few pieces that she'd been able to buy back from the pawn shops, and other items that James had sold off when he needed cash, she was saddened by how little there was. It had taken a while to gather what she had been able to. Nearly all the silver that had been monogramed for her and John on their wedding date had been found. She'd even managed to get most of the tapestries, as well as some of the linen that her grandmother had made centuries ago. And mostly all of the furniture. It had been the easiest to track down. Most people had no idea what they'd gotten from James's stupidity, and she'd been able to get it for far less than she could have imagined.

But some of the treasures that they'd had were never going to be found or used again. All the dishes and pottery that had been given to them, and things from her past were shattered and left in ruin at the back of the house. Marissa had surmised that he'd taken it outside and thrown it against the castle simply because he could. Her gowns, too, and his father's things, had been torn to shreds and had laid in the yard so long that they had become a part of the earth.

Touching her fingers to the portrait of her mother and father, she cried for what he'd done to their things. She knew that it really wasn't her fault. They'd all tried their best to curb his appetite for destruction and mayhem, even going to far as to send him abroad to places that dealt with children and adults like her son.

But that had been another huge mistake. Not only had he not learned anything there, but she was sure that was where he'd gotten his first taste of sex the way he liked it.

James was a sadist. He hurt women, nearly killing them, and her family had been made to pay his fines that were ordered by the council. But James hadn't stopped there. He'd come home when kicked out of the country, and hurt women and sometimes men with depravity. Marissa cried for the things that he'd put them through.

It was as if he were possessed with something. Evilness oozed from his pores, and it only got worse the older he got. Then he'd killed his father. Bragged about it to her. Telling her that he'd not begged for his life, not said a word to him, only that he'd get his comeuppance someday. That, she thought, had pissed him off more than his inability to kill her in the same manner.

"Oh, John, I miss you so much. You would have known what to do about him." She moved to lie upon the bed that she'd managed to take from the castle in her preparations to leave there. Some of her things had been put in this cave long ago for just this part of the journey to save herself from her son. "He killed any kind of love I might have had for him the day he took your sword from this house and used it upon you."

Feeling sorry for herself didn't solve anything, she knew this. But that was all that she had at the moment. She didn't miss the servants or the nice things that she'd had as much as she missed her son Griffith and the joy that he'd bring to her. She missed stepping out into the sunlight as her dragon, taking to the skies when the weather was just right enough to shield her. She missed being herself, too.

Marissa woke up and the cave was dark. But there was something with her, something in the cave where she'd been for all these years. Trying to find a place to hide, she made her way to the back of the cave and tried very hard to blend into the stones around her. But as she'd not been out, getting heat from the sun and the fresh air that a dragon needed, she wasn't well enough to completely disappear.

"Look, there are some of your mother's things here." Her first thought was that James had found her. He was going to kill her. "Griff, I think that you're right. She is alive and living here."

"Griffith?" She came out of her hiding place and lit up the cave with her magic. The two men standing before her were like a balm to her otherwise broken heart. "Oh, Griffith, I've missed you so very much. And Danburn, it's so wonderful to see you again."

She and Griffith embraced several times, their declarations of love tumbling over and over what the other was saying. He asked her why she was here, told her how much he'd missed her. Griffith, her loving son, was here, and she could not let him go.

He held her to him as he sobbed that he had missed her so very much. That he understood why she'd left when she had. Griffith even told her about his mate, one that she'd be so happy to meet, he told her. Danburn cleared his throat—the young man was king now, and Marissa bent on her knee before him, begging his forgiveness for not doing so sooner.

"You are like a second mother to me, Lady Farley. Please, stand." She did, then hugged him tightly as well. He was like her son too; he and Griffith had always had a special bond. "You are well then? Do you need anything?"

"Nay, I'm all right here. I've hated to be so close yet not

able to see my son. This mate of yours, she is good to you?" Griffith seemed to light up with the question. "I can see that she's made you very happy indeed."

"She has, Mother. Christ, I have missed you." She hugged him again, holding onto the only love that she'd missed more than her husband's. "James is causing trouble, as you can well imagine."

"I didn't mean to harm you that day, Griffith. You have to believe me. I thought it was him. I'd been out feeding my dragon and I saw him and the truck coming at me, and I didn't realize it was you until it was nearly too late." He told her that he understood. "You believe me?"

"Of course I do. You're my mother." She couldn't get enough of him. Just being with him, and him understanding what had transpired, was more than she could have hoped for. "Will you come home with us? I'd like nothing more than to take you to meet Lilac. Danburn has a new baby too."

"I cannot. Not with your brother out there." Griffith said that he'd not harm her again. "But he will. He has. What would happen if I were to go with you to stay in your lovely home and he came for me? I couldn't live with myself should another person that I loved be harmed by him. No, I can't do that to you."

"Danburn and I will protect you, Mother. And Kip, Dana, and well as the rest of the old gang is around as well. He will never harm you again—not so long as I live will he harm my family again." She leaned her head on his chest, wondering how she could convince him that she was doing this for him. "Lilac is a water faerie. She's the queen of the waterways. I am her king."

She looked at him then, just now noticing the difference in him. He was stronger than when she'd left, happier too, she could see. And his strength was great, even more so than she was.

Stepping back from him, Marissa noticed other things about him too. His eyes, so green before, were now a green so dark that they looked almost black. Even his height was different, his muscles stronger. Taking another step back from him, she asked to see his dragon.

The shift from man to dragon was immediate. There hadn't been any hesitation on his part as she might have thought he'd have. But when he was fully dragon, she saw that he was right—that Griffith could not just keep her safe, but all of them.

Marissa looked at Danburn when he laughed. She asked him what was so funny.

"He's changed in the last few days, my lady. His dragon is larger than before. His armor is also stronger. Griff always had a dangerous helmet, but now it looks evil, like it could do more harm than even I could if pushed. Yes, I do believe that should your other son come to him to cause any of you harm, he will have a reckoning that will haunt him for the rest of his days."

She believed it too. And when he laid his head down and put out his hand for her, she rubbed her cheek along his sharp claw and closed her eyes. His father hadn't lived long enough to see what their son had become.

Tears filled her eyes then, causing them to race along her face like a dam had been opened. When he asked her what was wrong, she told him—told him how proud his father would have been of him.

"I love you, Mother. Please, come home so that I might care for me. I will keep you safe, this I promise you." Marissa told Griffith that she believed him, but was no less frightened of James. "He will die by my hand if he so much as touches your hand. I will not allow him to hurt what is mine. Not ever again."

~*~

Lilac liked her new mother-in-law, but Marissa was as unsure of her role in the house as Lilac was. When they were left alone, Griff being called away for an emergency, she asked the older dragon to join her in the kitchen. It was the place she enjoyed most in the big house.

"We used to come to the kitchen, too, when we wanted comfort. Do you do that as well?" Lilac told her that she liked to cook some. Not a great deal. "Oh, that's wonderful. I never learned. And when I was on my own for so long, I promised myself that I'd learn something. Even boiling water was a trial for me. I would forget that I'd put it over the fire and nearly burn the pan to cinders, along with the logs."

"I, too, was on my own for a long time. However, since I can only be what I am, I didn't have the need to feed someone as large as your dragon would be. But still, not being able to be in the sunlight would have rendered my magic void. Even being what I am, I need the sunlight as much as I do the water. Danburn has allowed me to swim in his lake. It's very nice." She pulled out the things to make some salad. It was the only thing that she really loved to eat, besides some of the sweets that had been made by their cook.

"I'm not sure what I'm to do." Lilac smiled at her and told her that she felt the same way. "This is your home, yours and Griffith's, so I know that I'm not in charge. But it's also difficult for me, since I've been gone for so long, to know the proper way for things to be done."

"There is no proper way, Marissa. None at all. And I'd like for you to be yourself. If you see something that needs taken care of, we can work on it. I've not been in charge of a household before, and it's a bit overwhelming, I think." The other woman nodded and looked relieved a little more. "I'm helping with a

89

few projects that Elissa is on. She's been very helpful in showing me the ropes, so to speak. And the other women of the family, as she calls them, have been very nice to me as well. Have you seen the new baby?"

"Not yet. I'm to understand that you're going to have them all over for dinner tonight to see me. I've spoken to Elissa, and she cannot say enough good things about you and my son." She looked away, then back at her. "I'm going to tell you how sorry I am about James. I know some of what he had done to you, and I need you to understand that we did not raise him to be such a monster."

"I know that you didn't." She didn't look convinced, so Lilac set the salad that she'd made in front of her and joined her at the table. "James is running out of places that will accept him. And he's stealing from the local stores as well. Griff has been reimbursing them for what he takes because he doesn't want James to resort to killing people for food, so this is safer, we think."

"He killed his father. Did you know that?" Lilac told her that she did, that Griff had told her. "He was going to kill me as well. He'd been...well, I knew that I was next on his list, and I had started a rumor that dragons could be killed by feeding them iron. It would have taken him several decades of doing it that way, but the rumor that I started just for him said that it would be quick. Then I disappeared."

"That must have been very hard for you. I mean, to just leave everything that you loved behind to keep yourself safe." Marissa nodded and started to cry. "No one blames you for leaving. Especially Griff. You had to do what you needed to be safe. And from my experience with James, it would take drastic measures to do that. He's a monster. I'm sorry to say that, but...."

"No, you're right. And I don't even know why he's like that. We raised them the same. Treated them no differently when they were growing up. Griff was easier for us, I will admit that. James, it seemed, went out of his way to be mean and combative. For a long time, we thought that he was just jealous of Griffith. But I realized, too late, that he was just as you said, a monster." Lilac handed her a tissue when she cried harder. "I just don't know what to do. I know that he will continue his ways until someone kills him or puts him in prison. But even that, I don't think, will do any good. He's very resourceful and strong. Not as strong as you have made Griffith, but he won't stop until he gets all that he wants. And the really sad part of that is, I don't think he even knows what he wants. Just all of it, is all I can figure. He wants it all."

"Griff told me that he all but destroyed your family home. He's working to have some of the things that he'd found put back, and what has been damaged, he's working to get it repaired. He was so glad that you'd been able to save a great deal of it. I think they're moving it back today." Marissa said that was what she'd heard as well. "I guess they're going to make a showing of it too. Just to show James that he hasn't won a damned thing. I don't think that'll go over well, but it might be enough to get him caught."

"Then what will happen to him? Has anyone said? Because to be honest, Lilac, I don't care if he's put in irons for the rest of his days or killed. He's taken so much from everyone, and my love too." Lilac told her that she was so sorry about that. "As am I. I never thought, never in all my wildest dreams, that he would do something like that. To kill his own father. And for what? Money? The castle? He was going to get all that anyway. Why did he feel the need to rush it along?"

"Only he'll be able to tell us that." Lilac thought about

91

James. "I don't think he'll feel as if he needs to have a reason for anything that he's done or is about to do. He just feels...I guess you could call it deserving. The way that he took me, tied me to a tree and expected me to stay there and wait for his return, made me realize that James isn't normal and I'm not sure that I'd call him insane, but he isn't normal. And had it not been for my faerie friends, I think that I would be dead now." Marissa said again that she was sorry, and Lilac told her that it was all right. She had escaped and found her other half. "For a great many people it didn't work that way. I'm counting myself lucky to have been in a position that I could escape him. There are so many that weren't able to. And he will pay for that."

"Yes—soon too, I hope. And I can't help but worry that he's plotting a way to get to you again right now. Or Griffith." Lilac put her hand over hers and smiled. "You're so very kind to me, Lilac. I'm so happy that you're a part of Griffith's life. You've made him smile. And that, in my book, makes you perfect for him."

Blushing, Lilac thanked her. They had a lot of things to do today, and she was glad that they'd been able to talk. Sometimes, she knew, just talking to someone else made you feel like you could conquer anything you set your mind to. Something occurred to Lilac as she as finishing up her meal.

She'd not thought once of dying or ending her life. Before Griff, at least a two or three times a day, she'd think about ending her life or having someone put her to rest. Not because of anything that she'd done, but simply that she'd been around for so long, seen so much, that she'd resigned herself to thinking that it was never going to be better. That life as she'd known it was gone, and there wasn't any point in trying to change any of it. Humans were so sad in that. Like they didn't care about what they had but what they could get. Much like James was, but to a higher degree.

The furniture arrived at the castle just as she was getting ready to go over to see Elissa. Lilac had brought Marissa with her, just to make sure that things were put in the same places that they'd been before. And while there, she also made a list of things that had to be replenished, such as linens for everyday use, kitchen items and such. As well as a staff.

She and Griff had talked it over last night, and they were going to ask his mom to stay at the castle. It was a place where she'd feel comfortable, and she'd love being home. He had made sure that James could not get on the grounds by talking with the witch, Lady Beatrice. She had put a spell on the land and the castle that would keep even the most determined people out, thus keeping all those there safe as well.

Marissa was just directing where her bed went when Lilac saw James. He didn't come any closer to the land, but stood just beyond it in the place that was the shortest distance from the forest. James stared at them while they worked, and Lilac wondered if his mother had even realized that he was there. Not wanting to ruin her good mood, Lilac reached out to Griff and told him what was going on.

Are you worried that he could harm you? She said that she wasn't, just wanted to let him know that he was aware of the castle being loaded up and that his mom was there. *I wish I could hear what he's thinking right now. I bet he's as pissed as I've ever seen him.*

I would imagine he's plotting a way to get to the castle and us. Especially your mom. Speaking of which, I don't think she's noticed him yet. I hope that she doesn't. She's in such a wonderful mood. Griff said that he was on his way there with Kip. The two of them were working on his castle today. *The faeries said that they'd help him. I forgot to tell you. They miss being able to go inside of it too.*

93

Tell him if he were to call on Sunny, she'd be able to get him whoever he needs.

That's very kind of them. I'll let him know. But in the meantime, before we get there, I want you to keep an eye on James. I don't know what he'll do, but he won't just go away. Not now that he knows that Mom is around. She agreed with him, telling him that she'd keep her safe. *I know you will, love. I worry about both the ladies in my life.*

You're a goofball. They both laughed, and she felt rather than saw that James was coming toward them. He had something like a scent that told her to be wary of him. *He's coming toward us. And while I'm not worried, I'm just letting you know. I can kick his immortal ass all over the place if he fucks with me.*

Just be careful. I know I don't have to say this to you, but don't turn your back on him. He'll stab you so quickly that you'll never see it until it's too late.

Lilac promised him that she had this, and turned to look at James when the magic around the place stopped him. Joining him on the other side of the magic, Lilac thought that they'd lure him into getting himself in trouble. As well as a great deal of pain.

"What the fuck are you doing here? I thought you were told to stay the hell away from me. And if not, then stay the fuck away from me." He grinned—it looked purely evil. "Go away, James, before you bite off more than you'll be able to chew."

"You're mine. While I don't know your name, I've claimed you as my own. You'll—" She knew the exact moment that he saw his mother. Glancing at her to make sure that she was all right, Lilac looked back at James. He looked like someone had taken away his favorite dessert then dumped it on his fucking head. "What the fuck is this? You're supposed to be dead. You lied to me?"

He sounded so incredulous that she had to laugh. And that turned his temper onto her. Not that she gave a shit who he was pissed off at. She figured that she had the upper hand and wasn't going to take shit from him any longer. Marissa spoke with a great deal of humor in her voice as well.

"What did you expect me to do, James? Roll over and die, just for you? No, I don't think so. You'll pay for what you've done, and I'm going to make sure of it." He lunged at them both, but neither of them moved. There was too much magic in place around Lilac and the castle for him to do anything more than hit the solid wall-like magic. His mom laughed again. "Always so childish. I have no idea why you ever thought that you could pull a fast one on me. I'm a great deal smarter and stronger than you ever will be."

"You think so? Well, this is over. You're going to pay for lying to me. All this time, you've been lurking in the corners. You're probably the one that let loose this cunt too, aren't you?" Marissa looked at her then back at her son. "Well? Did you?"

"I'm sorry, but I don't understand. There's someone here that you think is a cunt? I don't see anyone that might even resemble that description. If you mean your sister-in-law, that's very rude of you, James. What do you think Griffith will say when he finds out that you are calling his mate by terrible names?"

"Mate? Fuck no. She's mine. I saw her first." Lilac said that he'd kidnapped her. "Well, so? You're just lucky that I didn't kill you like the others. I want you to come with me right now and we'll have us some fun. Griffith won't care once he finds out that I've had you before him."

"No, you didn't. And you're stupid if you think he'd believe you. In the event that you've forgotten, I'll remind you. Scent, you fucking idiot. He didn't smell you on me, so he knows for a fact that you're a fucking distrustful asshole."

"Distrustful? How can you stand there and call me that when you've both lied to me? You ran off. To me that's the same thing. I had plans for you. And what did you do? You fucked those all up for me, didn't you?" James looked at his mother. "And you. You fucking bitch, why the hell aren't you dead? I know for a fact that I killed you. Yet here you stand, acting like there isn't a thing wrong with it. You two are going to pay dearly for fucking with me."

When he drew back his fist, neither she nor Marissa moved. They were inside the magic while he wasn't this time. And when he screamed in pain, Lilac laughed when Griff took him to the ground. James cursed and called them both names that she was sure he was making up as he went along. And the things that he said about his own mother made her skin crawl. But through it all, Marissa stood there staring at him as if she'd never seen him before. Perhaps, and this might just be her, she'd never seen this side of James before.

When he was let go, he reached for Lilac and was burnt by the magic that surrounded her. The extra precaution that she'd put around them, she and Marissa, before leaving the house was paying off. His screams could be heard as he ran off, cradling his hand in his other one and threatening that he'd be back. She surely hoped that he would return. She'd kill him when he did.

Chapter 7

Griff was trying his best not to go out, find James, and kill him. Right now, he'd gladly go to the council and tell them that he was all right with spending the rest of his days in their prison. Anything to get this madman out of their lives. When his mom came to sit next to him on the couch he smiled at her, and when she laughed, he knew that she could see right through him.

"He's going to have to be put down like a dog." Mom nodded and said that someone should have done it long ago. "Yes, had I known what sort of.... That's not true. I knew just what sort of monster he was. I just found it easier to keep away from him rather than try to deal with him."

"When he said those things to me, all I could think about was I was so glad that your father wasn't here to see him. He knew what he was too, I'm sure, but the way James talked to me and about your lovely mate, I have to tell you son, I was hard pressed not to shift and take him out with my dragon." He told her that he'd been ready to do that as well. "I'm glad that you didn't. I don't know what sort of nightmares he's created for you, but I think it would bother you as much as it would me to kill him. I don't like him, and I've decided today, seeing him like that, I don't even love him anymore. He's just not right in the head."

"Danburn was pissed off too. I mean, you should have heard him cursing when we were making our way to you. I was sure that given the chance, he'd kill him without ever feeling a thing. It disturbed him greatly that James said that he was pissed because you weren't dead." Mom said that it had her as well. "Danburn is going to talk to the council about him. They don't have much say in his actions because he's not a dragon. But he thinks he can make a case with him killing Father and trying to do the same to you. That alone might get him into enough trouble that he can be imprisoned for a long time."

"I have a feeling that nothing will hold him. I don't know why I think that, but I believe that there isn't a cell strong enough to keep him from hurting others." In that moment he thought of Carmine, little sister to Quinn and daughter to Hanson. How she had taken care of other dragons. He needed to talk to Hanson and Cassie, to see what they thought about all this. Griff looked at his mom when she laughed. "You zoned out for a moment there. Are you all right?"

"Yes. Now that I have you here, I most certainly am." He held her hand in his and knew that for as long as he lived, he would never forgive James for taking her away from him. "Have you decided whether or not you'll stay in the castle? I assure you that you're more than welcome here. Lilac would love to have you here as well."

"Honestly, it's all I can think about, where I should lay my head. I'd so love to be at the castle—your father and memories of him are there. But again, there are a great many memories that hurt me as well." Griff told her that he understood. "Yes, I do believe that you would. He was a great man, your father.

98

And I loved him with every beat of my heart."

"I know that feeling as well." He looked over at his lovely Lilac as he continued. "She is everything that I had ever hoped for in a wife. Smart, a smartass, as well as someone that doesn't let anyone beat her down. I think that is why I love her the most — she can take me on and not have a bit of trouble about it. I think now, if James were to take her, he'd have his ass handed to him in a heartbeat. She doesn't have to hide now. Lilac can be what she needs to be."

"I do believe you're right on that one." They both laughed and Lilac turned to wink at him. "She's in love with you as well. I'm so happy that I could have witnessed you being in love. Your father, he would have been overjoyed with her. And love her as much as I do right now. She's good for you."

"I know. She makes me want to be a better man and a stronger dragon." He glanced at his mom and saw that she was still looking at Lilac. "She loves you as well, Mother. Very much so."

"I can feel it. I can. She's going to give you strong children, and ones that will be greatly as you are. Kind and yet strong at the same time." His mom put her hand on his leg and smiled. "I hope that I'll be around when you have your children. This is all that I ever wanted for you. A happy life."

"You'll be here. I promise you that. Nothing will harm you so long as I can keep you safe. As for James, he's going to make a major mistake. And when he does, I will bring a hurt down on him that he'll remember for the rest of his days. Which, I'm hoping, won't be all that long." His mom laughed with him and Lilac came to sit with them. "I was just telling my mom about how we'd like for her to stay with us, but if she wanted to go to the castle, that was good too."

"Yes. Either place you decide to stay, we won't ever be that far apart. Griff can get us there in no time at all. And being what I am, it wouldn't be difficult for me to visit you as well." Mom hugged both of them then sat back on the couch. "You're going to be all right; you know this, don't you?"

"I do. Now, anyway. I feel as if I can conquer the world without any trouble." Mom laughed again. "Of course, I'd have to get healthier first. My dragon has been without for too long. A few more days of just being in the sun and I'll be as fit as I've ever been."

Griff escorted the both of them to dinner when it was called. There was much to celebrate; a new babe, his mother being home, and a wife that he loved very much. Things that Griff never thought to have after his mom had supposedly died.

Dinner wasn't formal tonight. The things that he and Lilac had picked up at the auction had been cleaned and put in this room. Even the dishes, the ones that they'd gotten so cheaply, were in the cabinet now and gleamed beautifully.

The glasses had been a perfect match to the dishes. And in some of the boxes that they'd gotten cheap with the glasses, they'd found pieces of pottery that were old, and a few pipes that his father would have loved. As well as some jewelry, which looked old as well, that had been hidden away in a box in a false bottom.

He was telling his mom about the auction when Hoke came into the dining room. It was unusual in that he rarely came into the house, much less in the dining room. Griff knew something was wrong as soon as he took his hat off and bowed before them.

"What is it?" Hoke smiled and it did relieve some of the apprehension, but Griff was still worried. "Has something happened, Hoke? Tell me, I can take it."

"Nothing horrible, my lord. The barn—the faeries, they've

done a grand job of cleaning it up and repairing it. They did go a mite overboard on the painting, but I have to admit, I love it too." Relaxed now, he asked him what it looked like. "I'm sure you can see it from here, my lord. It's certainly bright enough."

Going to the window, he looked in the direction of the barn. Before he could spot it, he heard Lilac laughing, then his mother. When Griff saw the big building, he laughed as well. They had used every color imaginable to make it stand out.

"Are those flowers that they've painted there?" Hoke told his mom that it was. "They're very well done, if a little large." Deciding to get a better look, they stepped out onto the porch and stared at the building. "My goodness, there will be little doubt as to finding it in the winter months now."

They returned to the dining room, with the plans to go out to see it later. Griff was still laughing about it when dessert was served. Even thinking about how he'd missed it at first made him feel good. The barn was a great reflection of the way he felt about life in general now.

"I'm going to live in the castle, if you're sure you won't mind." He and Lilac both said that they didn't. "I only just realized that it's where I need to be. I want to be there to be able to talk to my John, live out the days I have there in the home that belonged to my family for generations. If you will promise me one thing—when you have a child of your own, you come to your home to give birth, and let your children come to visit me when possible."

"Deal." Lilac looked at him when he laughed at her. "What? You think she'd do a horrible job at it? Or is it that you think she will spoil our children rotten? I, for one, hope that she does. Every child should be spoiled by their grandparents. And she has to make up for both of them."

"I was just hoping that you'd allow me to tell her yes, that's all." Lilac told him he needed to be quicker if he wanted to keep up with her. "I'm beginning to see that. But yes, I agree with you. Mom should be able to spoil them as much as she wishes. And I do hope that she'd want them to come and stay with her. It would only be fitting for her to tell our children all about what a goof, as you're so fond of calling me, their father is."

"Oh, son. I have a long list of things that I could tell them. And have fun too." Mom laughed, and Griff realized how much he'd missed that when he thought she was dead. "You should come over sometime, Lilac. I could tell you stories that would have you calling him more than a goof. He was a good boy most of the time, but there were times.... Well, you come to tea sometimes and I'll fill you in. It would be my pleasure."

They were all still laughing as they went up to bed that night. Mom was going to go to the castle in the morning to make a list of some of the things that she'd still need. He was heading into town to see about getting both he and Lilac a new car, and to set up with the faeries to keep the castle in tip top shape for his mom. He grieved for a moment about his truck but decided this was good too. They both could use something larger. Griff didn't think that his life could get any better than it was at this very moment.

Now, all he had to do was deal with his brother and he could move on. And so could everyone else. Yes, he thought, the sooner this was finished with James, the better off the whole world would be.

~*~

James paced back and forth in the valley where he'd been staying. The caves above him were off limits to him for some reason. Well, he knew the reason—his brother again. Or his mother. The nerve of her going behind his back and faking her death. The more he thought about it, the angrier he got. The

102

fucking bitch had let him believe she was dead. How deceitful could a person get?

"At least I'm honest about what I do. I'm going to kill her. And make sure that she's dead this time too. Then I'm taking care of Griffith. I've had enough of all of them." He looked at his pitiful living arrangements. "Fuckers have made me sleep with the fucking animals."

He'd been able to take a tent, but the instructions were all fucked up and he wasn't able to make the thing work. So now it lay over a small tree to keep most of him dry when it rained, but he still got wet whenever the clouds opened up.

"While I know that they have nothing to do with the rain, I have a funny feeling that they have a little to do with it. Why the hell is it raining every fucking day?" He wondered if it was raining everywhere and not just over him, but he didn't have the strength to go into town again to find out. "They've made it so I've had to move as far from the town as a few miles. I don't know who the they are, but you can bet that I'm going to get them too."

The last trip he'd made to town had cost him nearly a day of time. James had not been in good shape any part of his life, and now was no different. The walks that he'd been taking to even get a little food were making him so exhausted that he could barely think of a good plan, much less have the energy to carry them out. And that was their fault as well.

His mother was alive. Christ, that wasn't right. He'd done just as he'd been told. Of course, he'd had no idea at the time that she'd been the one leading him down that merry path of wrongness, but she should have been more honest with him. James laughed at himself.

"Yes, you idiot, she's going to tell you how you made so many mistakes in trying to kill her off. I'm sure that she's going to break it down so that you can do a better job next time." He laughed again, feeling the bitterness of it as the anger seemed to wrap around his body. "That was just wrong. Wrong on so many levels, to let me think that I was killing her off. At least with my dad, I knew that he was dead. His head looking up at me, that was proof enough for me."

Pacing more, happy that he could hear the rodents and other animals scurrying to get out of his way, he thought of that woman. Still he had no idea what her name was, and that burned him more than anything. To think that she'd gotten away from him and gone straight to his brother. There was no justice in the world, he thought, when his own fucking brother had it better than he did.

"I'm going to make him pay for that too." James was getting confused about what he was supposed to be making Griffith pay for. Some days it was that he'd had it better than him. Other days he would be pissed off because he had James's woman. And even on some days, he wanted him to pay simply because he'd been born at all. "I should have been an only child. Then I would have gotten it all without him sticking his nose into my business."

He could see the castle from where he was and knew what was going on there. Just yesterday he'd seen the trucks and vans pull up in front of it, with large signs on them that said things like carpet cleaners, glass repairs, and even one that had safe installation. Like there was anything left in the place to keep inside one.

But as he continued to watch from a distance, he saw things going into the castle that he knew for a certainty that he'd sold off or simply destroyed. Tapestries that he had sold for money were being cleaned and then taken in. There were the beds that he'd given away or pawned. This shit was making him crazy, wondering who the hell had told them they could replace things that he'd deemed unworthy of keeping.

"Like any of them ever listened to me. But they will soon enough. Listen to me as I cut their lives short and make a stew from their skin." He knew that as dragons they were worth a great deal. But so far he'd not been able to get anything from anybody that he'd been around. Even his asshole brother had been careful not to leave any part of himself around. A fucking scale alone would have been enough to set him up for a couple of years.

"But no, he's as selfish as I am about that shit." Even when they were children, Griffith had taken care that he'd pick up his own scales and put them in the lakes around their home. And any blood that he might have shed, it too was put to use in the forest, giving enough of himself to make them grow to great heights, with more health than they might have needed. "Griffith should have shared it with me. Should have been willing to give me what I wanted. I'm the oldest and shouldn't have to live like this. Like a squatter on land that I should own."

Pacing more, he stopped by a tree and watched the deer that were always out this time of the evening. His mouth watered when he thought of having a nice deer steak, or a few other treats that he couldn't find in the wooded areas. But they, too, were out to kill him. Whenever he was close enough to shoot them with his hand gun, they seemed to know when he was ready to take them down and would run off. He was sure they were laughing at him too.

The lake that was near enough that he could fish to get a meal didn't help either. He had no way to catch them, even should he have known how; a pole and string, and whatever else that was needed, eluded him. Nothing at all was going his way. And he was getting mighty sick and tired of it.

He looked down at the stones he'd put in a circle three days ago. So far, with all the rain, all he'd managed to do was have a roaring smoke out. Never a spark of a flame nor anything to keep him warm. James wondered if there was a time in his life that he'd been as cold and wet as he was right now. Shivering again, he sat down on the wet blankets he had under the soaking wet broken down tent.

Screaming out his frustrations, James wanted to cry. This was not the way he thought things should be going for him right now. He should be living in the castle that Griffith had cleaned up. He should have clean clothing, a nice fire in the hearth, and food at his beck and call whenever he wanted it. All he had for being born first was a pile of wet clothes — no food or clean water. And he couldn't light a fire to save his life.

He thought of his father the day before he'd killed him. Smiling, he remembered like it was yesterday his dad telling him that he had plans of changing the way things were going. That he wished for Griffith to have the castle when they left there, as neither he nor his mother had any confidence in him keeping it the way it had been for generations.

"You can't take that from me. It's mine, I tell you. You can't do that." Father had told him that not only could he, but he'd already asked the dragon council if it could be done. "Why the fuck do you think that I'd allow you to do that? I'm the first born, and I'm wholly sick and tired of having to beg for every little thing that I want."

"Beg for what, James? You've had everything that you wished provided for you. A home, servants, money when it wasn't too much. You have lived a relatively good, easy life. How do you think you're owed more than that?" He said that he wanted the castle given to him now. "Nay, I've told you. We're not going to leave it to you. You've taken much of what

106

was there anyway. It's time that you made your own way in the world."

"I am making my way in the world. I just don't do it as you have. I want it now, Father. You've no right to take from me what doesn't belong to you. I want any money that you've stashed away, as well as for you to turn the castle over to me. Its mine by right of birth." His father had only shaken his head. "You will do as I say, Father, or you'll pay dearly for it."

"What will you do, James? Kill me? Go ahead and try. But you won't get away with it should you succeed. I'm master of the house, and you will heed my warning that you're going to have to make your own way in the world."

The next day, James had waited in the woods surrounding the castle for his father to take his daily walk. And when he'd come upon his father, he drew the sword that had hung over the mantle for decades. A sword that had been presented to his father by Damn Bird's father, for his help in the wars.

"You've pissed me off, Father dear, and I want you to tell me that you'll stop this nonsense about taking the castle from me and turn it over to me now." Father told him no, it was done. "No. It isn't done until I say so. Beg me, Father, to allow you to live and I might. Or I might not. I don't know at the moment."

"Do you think you could get away with killing me, James? Do you think that no one will care that you've murdered your own sire? I have news for you should you succeed in killing me, I can guarantee that you'll get what's coming to you. You'll get your comeuppance sooner than you think." He laughed at his father as he ordered him to his knees. As he went down, his hands at his sides, James felt the anger that had been building since yesterday roll over him like a deluge. He screamed at him to beg him. "Nay, I will not. Do what you must but know that someday you're going to be brought to heel, and then I will have a peaceful death knowing that you've been killed too."

The sword was too heavy for him. But with his anger, swiping it through his father's neck seemed easy, too easy. And when nothing seemed to have happened, because his father was still intact, he leapt back when his father laughed as his head fell from his shoulders and landed right in front of James, his smiling face looking up at him from the ground. It was too much, and instead of picking up the body and taking it back to the castle for his mother to see, James ran away, terrified that his father would come back to life and kill him.

Chapter 8

Griff stood in the shower and let the water roll over him. If he was honest with himself, which he usually was, he'd say that he was too old for this shit. Laughing at himself, he reached up for the shampoo just as the door to the shower stall opened.

"Hello there." He reached for Lilac as she made her way to him. "This is just what I needed. You washing my back."

"I have something else in mind. I was thinking that I'd take your cock into my mouth and swallow you down." He nearly fell on his ass when Lilac wrapped her hand around his hard cock. "Unless you'd rather I washed your back for you."

"No, you do what you must. I'll try and suffer — Holy fuck, Lilac. That's it."

She was on her knees before he could finish his sentence and held him hostage in her mouth before he could brace himself for her touch.

All thoughts went out of his head. She used him as one would an all-day lollipop, and he couldn't seem to catch his breath. When she moaned, he looked down at her as she bobbed on his cock and saw that in his stupor of being taken this way he'd crushed the shampoo bottle, and the creamy liquid was filling the stall with bubbles.

Turning off the water was harder than he thought it would be. When she cupped his balls in her hand and held them tightly but gently, he felt his eyes roll to the back of his head and stay there. Reaching down to...well, he wasn't sure what his plan had been, but as soon as he cupped the back of her head, his cock exploded in his release.

Griff cried out as his balls filled again. He wasn't sure that he could stand much longer, surely not through another climax like that. Sliding down to the floor, even to be steady on his feet, seemed to be a feat that was well beyond what he was capable of at the moment. But she never stopped, didn't let him take a breath as she swallowed him past the tight muscles at the back of her throat.

Coming this time, he could only hold onto the wall. It was that or he was surely going to hit the floor. As she stood up, fisting his cock as she did so, Griff was sure that he was finished. There wasn't any way that he was going to be able to come again. But then she took his hard nipple into her mouth and bit down.

"Christ, you're killing me." Her laughter gave him a surge of energy, and he picked her up in his arms and took her to the bedroom. Dropping her on the bed, he followed her down and settled between her legs. "I'm going to make you pay, my dear."

"Yes, please. I'm so needy that I think I'll come the moment you touch me." He slid his fingers through the fine hair at her apex. She was soaking wet, the curls there were dewy with her obvious need, and when she begged him for more, Griff leaned down and took her fully in his mouth. Her scream pierced the room.

Her juices flooded his mouth. She caught him between her thighs as she rode his mouth. No matter how many times she came, and he'd lost count long ago, Lilac begged him for more, telling him with her body and her voice that she needed his all, everything that he had. Griff moved up her body, nipping and tasting her as he went.

The indentation of her navel seemed to hold secrets that he wanted to know. The way her ribs heaved in and out made him glad that he was seeing her this way. Lilac was beautiful. Sexy. He fell in love with her more with every beat of his heart, every breath that he took. And when he slid into her, his cock feeling her heat, her tightness around him, Griff could have gladly spent the rest of his days this way—Lilac beneath him, and him buried to the hilt inside of her.

Making love to her was easier now. Before, and all the other times that they'd come together, they both had been so needy, so ready to come, that it was difficult to enjoy each other. But they'd both had a fantastic release, several in fact, and now it was just for them.

"I love you, Lilac." She held him, her hands lazily going up and down his arms, his back. "You make me a better man every day that I'm with you. I love the way you feel when we make love."

"You make me want to be the best that I can be." He started to move, slowly making her his. "The way that you hold me, the way that you make love to me, it's wonderful. You're wonderful, and I love you more than words can say."

He kissed her then, tasting his release on her tongue. Griff found that he enjoyed that as much as he did her taking him. It was as if he was having her again and again. The taste of himself blending with her made him realize that they were one and would be for long after this day.

111

KATHI S. BARTON

Making love to her slowly was amazing. When she moaned, he felt it in her chest as it touched off strikes of lightning-like feelings in his heart and body. Every caress, hers to him, was like he was being touched by a live wire, his skin seeming to accept it as a token of her love. His dragon, begging for him to mark her before, seemed content with what they were doing.

"Take me, Griff. Make me yours."

At her words, strong and needy, he took her hard, filling her with each stroke, giving her another part of himself. And when she cried out, screaming his name as she came, he followed her, filling her with all that he had within him, until he felt the world turn and his heart stop beating for several seconds.

Waking up, not even sure when he'd fallen asleep in the big bed, Griff reached for Lilac, only to find her side of the bed cold. Her pillow, still smelling like her, had an indentation of her head, and Griff took it to his nose to smell her scent. Getting up, he reached for her, just realizing that it was well after noon and he'd been asleep for several hours.

I'm at the bank. Did you know that there are all kinds of things that you can invest in that are right here in this town? He told her that he'd been looking into that too. *I've decided to set up a scholarship fund for kids coming out of the local high school. I have the money, and I think that someone could benefit from it more than I could by just having my money sitting around in a jar.*

Do you really have your money in a jar? He turned on the water, thinking of the last time he'd stepped in there. *Please tell me that you don't.*

I do, as a matter of fact. I actually have it buried in different places around. Some in caves too. It's very useful to have it where I can get to it at a moment's notice. Sunny keeps track of it all, and when we need something, she and I will go there and get some. She laughed, and he smiled at the sound of it as he washed his hair. *I've had a*

112

few poachers over the decades, but I always figured that if they need it badly enough, then I did them a favor by leaving it behind. And sure, it could have been someone else, like your brother, who found it, but I like my version of it better.

And you call me a goof. I'm just getting out of the shower, for the second time today. How about you and I have lunch in town? Mom is finishing up having things arranged in the castle today, and told me that she was going to stay there from now on. Lilac told him that she'd talked to his mom that morning about meeting for dinner next week. *Good. I'd like that. And she'll be safe there too. Have you seen my brother around today? He's not going to be happy about any of this going on.*

He'll get over it. Or not. I don't care anymore. My mom is keeping an eye on him for us. She said that for the moment, he's taken refuge in a cave near the castle. But he's not doing anything but talking to himself. He felt her pause, thinking that she was speaking to someone else when she came back to him. Griff was just leaving the house when he realized that he didn't have a car any longer. The one that he'd ordered one for each of them, but they wouldn't be ready for a few more days yet. He was upgrading to something stronger. *Griff, you should get here soon. I'm not sure what is going on in town, but every shop on the main drag is closed up. I'm looking around now.*

I don't have a car. She asked him if he could get someone to bring him. *I'm sure that I can. I'll get one of the others to come for me. Unless you think that I need to get there right now. I can be there in a few seconds as my dragon.*

Yes, I think that would be a great idea. Her calmness wasn't very helpful. While he could feel her fear of something, it was the way that she was handling it that had him shifting immediately and heading to town. Griff asked the others to join him, not having any idea what was going on.

113

My mom is there now. She said that she was sitting in the diner when the place was starting to close up around her. Mom doesn't know what is going on either. We're all on our way. Griff thanked Danburn as he landed as his big dragon right outside of the town. Reaching to Lilac, he tried to think what the hell could be going on. *I can see you, Griff. Christ, it looks like they've all disappeared, doesn't it?*

As soon as they were men again, they ventured out onto the main street. When he saw Lilac, she came to him with Elissa and the other women. They all looked worried, and he was almost afraid of what might be going on.

"Look over there. The building there looks like it has lights on." Cautiously they made their way to it. Griff glanced at Kip when he spoke again. "It's like a ghost town. Kinda creepy, if you asked me."

"You're not helping." Kip just smiled at him and Griff wanted to ask him what the fuck was wrong with him. As they got closer to the building, he felt his dragon curl up, like he was ready to take him should he need it. Christ, this was scary as fuck.

Did his brother do this? Did he make all the shops in town close up and was holding the patrons hostage? He had no idea why, but his thoughts went to James lining up all the people and removing their heads one at a time. When Danburn was near the door, he wanted to tell him not to open it. Whatever was wrong, he could deal with it tomorrow or never.

"You stand there while I open the door. We'll have the element of surprise if we do this correctly." Danburn nodded to him as he stood on the side of the door where it would open. Griff didn't want to see what sort of carnage his brother had done. And when Danburn said, "Now," they all rushed into the building ready for whatever happened.

114

"Surprise!"

He barely held onto his dragon when all the townspeople jumped up and yelled at him. Happy Birthday signs were everywhere. So were balloons and other decorations. Griff sat down hard, glad that there had been a chair behind him when he did.

"You should have seen the look on your face." Danburn was laughing hard, and Griff wondered how hard he'd laugh if he knocked him on his ass. "You have no idea how difficult it was for me not to laugh in your face as you stood by the door. I wish I'd had a camera. It's a face I will never forget."

"You scared the shit out of me, you moron." Of course, instead of Danburn saying he was sorry, he laughed harder. Taking the drink from Lilac, Griff pulled her to his lap and held her while he soothed his terror with a glass of juice. "Did you plan this?"

"No. Elissa did. She said that she'd been planning it for a couple of months, and was so glad that I was able to celebrate with you. How old are you, anyway?" He had to think on that. Not having birthdays like other people did, he had to subtract the year he'd been born from the year it was now. "You have to think that hard on it?"

"Yes. I'm nine hundred and twenty-five years old." Lilac told him that it was small wonder that he could even move around, being so old. "Yeah? Well, my dear mate, how old are you?"

"Older than you by nearly three times." That startled him. He'd had no idea that there were beings older than Danburn. "Of course, like you, I've not thought about the years either. It's sort of depressing when you're all alone, isn't it?"

"Yes. But with you here, I feel younger than I have in decades. I didn't know that you were older than Danburn."

115

She told him that there were a lot of her kind that were older than even Danburn's mother. "I just realized that it's James's birthday as well. I can't remember the last time we celebrated together. I would guess it's been hundreds of years."

"Mother and I, we celebrate our birthdays by picking a large bouquet of flowers and sending them out to sea. The fishes are so happy to get them that we stand for hours while they disappear." Lilac kissed him on the mouth quickly as she stood up. "Come on now. I'm starving. You helped me burn off a lot of calories this morning."

The town had gone all out for his birthday. There were gifts, all of them handmade by them, that he knew that he'd cherish forever. There was plenty of food too; everyone was able to get their bellies filled, and enjoy plenty of drinks too.

Griff found Elissa and thanked her for the party. "It was my pleasure. I figured that with all this other crap going on, you and your mother could have a nice day of it. She's over there, near the cake." He saw her and smiled when she turned to him. "You're a very lucky young man — you know that, don't you? To have your mother after all this time, I'm so happy for you both. But what are you going to do about James?"

"I'm going to call him out and finish this. The council and my mom gave me permission to do what I must. Kip and Dana are going to be with me." She asked him why not Danburn. "James isn't a dragon, but the child of one. So if Danburn shows up at this, James could plead his case to him. I don't know what he'd say, but it would be drawn out more while James was able to call out witnesses on his behalf, as well as a written statement on why he shouldn't be imprisoned. This will get it finished quicker."

Elissa hugged him and then moved on. Lilac joined him then as they stood in line to grab some of the food. Griff was going to do this. Soon. It was well past time to take his brother down. And he had a feeling that it wasn't going to be nearly as easy as it sounded in his head.

~*~

James wandered around the little town after leaving his mother to her business. The thought of her living in his home made him so mad that he could barely contain himself. Smiling, James thought of the way that he'd been able to soothe himself. He'd managed to kill four people, heinously as his brother would call it, and he felt like a new man.

"Teach them to have a picnic close to where I'm residing." Like he was really residing in the caves. That too had burned his toast, as his father had been so fond of saying. "I live in a fucking forest, surrounded by all kinds of bugs and other shit."

James looked at his arms. They were covered in bite marks. Some of them he'd scratched raw. Even his legs looked as if he'd been laying in a hill of red ants. Which, he thought, was just what he'd done. The fuckers had bitten him so many times that his legs were more red and bloody than they were flesh. He wondered if his brother had anything to do with that, and decided to blame it on him anyway.

"He's going to get his soon." James had thought of and dismissed a great many plans to make his brother pay. None of them were very good. He had to keep reminding himself that his brother was a dragon, and if pushed too hard, would hurt him. "I have plans that will keep me going for some time, and having myself injured will not help me with that."

James wondered if Griffith's promise to their mother would still stand. She wasn't dead, so perhaps Griffith would now be able to hurt him. Since he was an immortal, there wasn't any way for Griffith to kill him, but he could definitely put him in a world of hurt.

"Would serve him right if he were to hurt me in a way that would require me to be bedridden, and he would have to care for me." That sounded like it would be fun. With the exception of the pain part. No one in their right mind would want to be in pain. "I love to inflict it, but never do I want to feel it. Having my hand busted up was enough for me."

The town seemed to be dead today. He noticed that several of the shops that he'd frequented were closed up, as well as the library. James wondered what the fuck was going on when he saw the building and the party going on. Stepping into the alley that gave him the best view, he watched as balloons were brought to the front of the place and a band set up nearby. Whatever was going on, it was a big hoopla. Getting closer, he could see now that it was some sort of birthday celebration.

"Probably Damn Bird having himself a party. The fucker never once invited me to any of his parties. Just Griffith." Watching the proceedings, he thought about birthdays and realized quite suddenly that it was his own birthday. Then it hit him. "Mother fuck, they're having a party for my brother. That should be for me, not him. I'm going to have to have a talk with him. The fucker didn't even remember to wish me a happy day."

Stalking his way to the building, he paused when he saw the other dragons there as well. They were men, of course, but he knew them all to be dragons. They had hung around his home often enough that he even knew all their names. From Damn Bird to the youngest of them, Kipling Newton.

The band started playing almost as soon as they got set up. "Happy Birthday" was sung by everyone there. James saw his mother there, holding onto Griffith like he deserved it. And he saw that she was singing the loudest, wishing her little boy a happy day.

James made his way to them now. He didn't have a plan, but he was going to have it out with them. To think that he'd not been invited to the party, nor had anyone bothered to wish him well today. Grabbing his mother's arm, James jerked her around so that she could see him.

"Mother dear, have you forgotten what day this is for me as well?" When she took a step back from him, his temper burned through him. But before he could reach for her the second time, his woman stepped between him and his mother. "You're coming with me. It's the very least that you can do for not having me a party as well."

Reaching for her, he grabbed thin air. He found himself lifted from the ground without anyone touching him. Screaming to be let go, that this was his birthday as well, he spit at his mother and the woman that had been taken from him.

"You seem to not understand that none of us like you, James." He started to spit on Damn Bird, but he laughed, a laughter that made James's skin crawl. "You spit again and I will tear out your tongue and shove it up that pansy ass of yours."

"Put me down this minute. You have no right to detain me like this. This isn't even your concern. This is between my mother and my mate." Damn Bird crossed his arms over his chest and it made James realize just how out of shape he was when he did that. "What the fuck do you care what is going on between us, you moron? You know as well as I do that you have no rights over me."

"That is where you're wrong, my dear asshole. When you kill a dragon, you immediately come under my rule. The council came to me just this morning, telling me that they'd ruled that you were to be treated like a dragon and I was to take care of you. How do you want to die, James? I'm all for stretching it

119

out for as long as I can, but I will give you the choice. But you will heed my word or face the consequences."

"You can't kill me, you fucking dick. I'm an immortal." He was let down to touch the ground, but he wasn't able to take a step. "If you persist in this, whatever you call it, in trying to make me heel, I have news for you—it won't work, Damn Bird. I'm not a part of your realm. I'm not a dragon, sadly, or you'd be toast right now. Christ, I fucking loathe you."

"Well, that's good. Because I'd hate to think that after all this time you'd fallen in love with me. Christ, that would be just shitty on your part, wouldn't it, Jiminy Cricket?"

James saw red. His temper just snapped and he tried to lunge at the man. But something was holding him, and he looked around for the source and eyed his woman.

"Let me the fuck go, and I'll make your death painless and quick. Not to say I'm not going to fuck you—I'm going to do that over and over—but after I'm finished, I'll just remove your head and be done with you." He laughed. "I might even not piss on your dead body if you were to let me go right now."

"I'm not holding you." She moved to her right and there stood a little girl. She couldn't have been much older than about ten or so. "This is Carmine, my niece by marriage. She's very strong, James—you should remember that when you fuck around with this family. And she doesn't have to touch you to know what you're thinking. Unlike you must do."

James knew that wasn't true. He could feel magic, and it wasn't coming from the child. Then she snapped her little fingers. The pain in his arm made him puke down the front of his shirt. He couldn't move away, couldn't even try and hold himself where the pain was coming from. Looking at it, he could see that it was broken in two places, the bones sticking out of his flesh like a bizarre art project.

"What the fuck have you done to me?" The child stepped to him. "You are going to fucking pay for this, see if you don't. And when I'm through with you, there won't be anyone that can recognize your fucking body."

Another snap of her fingers and his other arm was broken. Screaming at her around the pain, he was weak with the agony. When she looked up at him, no more than a few feet from his broken body, he wanted to reach out and snap her neck. But it was the expression on her face that made him think that saying or doing anything at this moment would not only get him killed, even being an immortal, but he'd be in a great deal of hurt until she ended his life.

"You're a horrible man." He whimpered; no sound other than that would make its way past his lips when Carmine spoke. "I would like nothing more than to send you away, but you need to suffer for what you've done."

"I am suffering, you little fuck. Fix me or else." She laughed, and it felt like nails on a chalkboard to him. "Let me go. Please, let me go and fix me."

"Nope. You're not nice, and if you're hurt like this, I want you to think about what else I could do to you for all the people that you've killed." Her hair danced around her head, and he felt the heat of her anger all over him, much like the breath of a dragon. The step she took toward him had him flinching away and causing more of him to hurt. "When you're dead, we'll all rest easier. You will suffer at the hands of those that you think should worship you — you will hurt worse than you ever have. And you will die by the one that you would least expect to be able to kill you."

He found himself in the forest again. James tried to sit up, to see what other hurts she'd bestowed onto his poor body. But without the use of his arms he was stuck there, lying like a turtle that had been turned to his back.

Sobbing about what he'd had to endure over the last few days, all he could think about was the pain. Pain that a child with no more magic than the rocks that he was uncomfortably lying upon. James didn't know what to do now. She had warned him, yes, but he knew that with her so young, there was little that she could do to someone as powerful as him.

"Just because she broke my arms doesn't mean that she can kill me. I'm a fucking immortal, and she'd better learn that people bigger and stronger than her will kick her human ass all over this place."

He laid there until the darkness came over his resting place. James didn't move any more than he had to. His pain tolerance, if someone would have asked him, was higher than most. But right now, he'd give anything for someone to knock him out, or to give him something for the pain. And somehow, he knew that it was going to take longer than it usually did for him to heal.

"You mother fucking bitch, you're not on my list." He cried some more, wondering why everyone seemed to be out to get him. "I'm firstborn to a very wealthy family of dragons. Why isn't anyone taking care of me? Why do they persist in making my life miserable like this?"

It wasn't until the sun was coming up again that he thought he could sleep. His mind was a jumble of activity in coming up with tactics. Every plan that he had and then rejected had to do with him killing his brother and his woman. But the child, and whatever she had in her arsenal, would cock block every move he came up with.

"I will get you, kid. You just wait and see if I don't." He tried to remember if there had been anyone there that looked as if they were helping her. "You have an entire dragon herd around you, and that is completely unfair. I'll even the odds the next time we meet. You can bet on that."

Just as he was falling asleep, he heard her laughter. It scared him so badly that he jumped, hurting himself more than he had in the last hour. Something else to add to what he was going to make them pay for. Haunting him while he tried to rest.

Crying himself to sleep didn't help his disposition any, but he was making progress, he thought, on getting healed. As soon as he found a way to get them, he was going to have them pay for everything that had happened to him. Even if they'd had nothing to do with it.

"Fuckers, every last one of them."

Chapter 9

The house was finished. Walking from room to room with Griff had her thinking of all the fun that they'd had going to auctions and finding pieces that they'd wanted. They were going to two this weekend and were hopeful of getting a few things to put in the storefront that they'd been planning.

"Do you really think that people will want to come to a shop like this? Just to look around?" They'd discussed it a great deal, opening a shop that didn't sell antiques but had them on display so that people could see how people used to get things done in a day's time. "I mean, I think it's a wonderful idea. But then, I'm happy to be doing anything with you."

"Thank you." Griff kissed her on her nose and smiled at her as he wrapped his arm around her. "I do think they'll come, actually. We both have things that we've collected over the centuries. I can see how it would appeal to a great many people to see uniforms of every decade. The swords and knives alone will be the highlight for every little boy within a hundred miles."

"And the plates that we've found, as well as the few

125

that we managed to keep, will be marveled at by most of the adults." While she was warming to the idea, she still had her doubts. "I saw some of the farmers around looking over the old steam engines when they were brought into town. One of the older men was telling his grandchildren how hard he'd had to work to keep the old plows going. Also, I heard from the other dragons; they're going to put a few things in it as well when we rotate some of the items out."

Danburn had been in favor of the museum of sorts. He was also glad that they were going to hire some of the people around town to be on hand to help with the tours that were being set up. And Elissa had been giving them smaller things with information cards with them for the last few days. If nothing else, when they first opened, Lilac figured that they'd have a lot of people coming by to see what they had.

"I think not charging anyone to come through is a good idea too." Lilac agreed with Griff as they made their way to the last bedroom down the hall. "This is the only room that needs a few things in it. The bed is perfect, and the canopy is one that my mother designed for it. I simply love it. But I think it needs a couple of wingback chairs. Just to sit by the fireplace."

"Good idea. And what did you think of the room next to this one? With all the babies coming along, when the others visit us, we'll have a place for the children as well. Did your mom have nannies for you, or did she care for you and James by herself?" She looked at him when he didn't answer. "I'm sorry, Griff. I didn't mean to make you upset."

"You didn't. I was just thinking about your question. My father was very hands on with me. Not so much James, as he wanted nothing to do with any kind of sports or play. Mom, she would be on the sidelines of every game I was playing in, dragging James along with her. He hated to be with us, and it finally got to the point where he'd just stay home, and we'd go on adventures without him."

"That must have been sad. Though, I don't know how. Not having James around to suck all the fun out of your trips might have been a good deal more inviting." She sat down on the bed and loved how it felt under her. It was a thick mattress, the kind that they'd have had during the time period of the bedstead. "Have you seen him lately? I heard from Rett that he's been in town a couple of times. Just to snatch up some food and return to wherever he's been staying."

"The grocery store had a list of things that he's swiped from them. Mostly it's been food, but he did get himself a few extras. I haven't any idea how he thinks he's getting away with this. But as of tomorrow, his stealing is going to come to a halt. They'll be watching for him after today and will have him arrested on sight if he does it. And let's be honest here, there isn't any way that he's going to stop. Not when he thinks that he's been getting away with it for so long." Griff laughed with her. "Yesterday I was told that he took several cans of beans. I would hate to be around him when they finally go through his system. Mr. Wells said that he took about fifteen cans of the stuff. He'll be a mess when he's finished with those."

Making their way down the stairs, the front doorbell rang as they were hitting the last step. Hoke had apparently been in the house, because he came from the kitchen area as soon as Griff started to open the door.

"No." Griff backed away from the door but stood close to it when Hoke warned him. "There are a few people around town looking for you. One of them is a woman, and I can't get close enough to her to figure out what she is."

"How do you know that it's them?" Hoke just pointed to his nose. Lilac was whispering, but she knew that both Hoke

127

and Griff could hear her. "So, do you pretend that we're not home? Or do we open the door and find out what the hell they want?"

"Wait, I think. It's better than having them come to your home to confront you, don't you agree?" She did, and so did Griff. "If I was you, sir, I'd just go about my way and leave them to whatever it is they want. I'll see what I can find out about them in town, and get back to you about it. Is that all right with you?"

Griff looked at her and she nodded. "Yes, it's fine with us both. But you be careful. A few days ago, Danburn told me that a woman was searching for me, by my titles. I'll get with him too, and see if he can shed some more light on this."

When the person knocked again, all three of them made their way to the kitchen. As with all dragon homes, the kitchen or hearth was the heart and warmest place in the house. Lilac had come to enjoy being in the big room too, even when the cook was away. Sitting at the table, she was given a large salad with grilled chicken on it. Also, a tall glass of tea. That was something else that she'd gotten used to, the sweet brew that was made daily for the household.

The person was gone by the time they had finished their lunch. Lilac had a lot of things to do today to get ready for their auction trip this weekend. Griff said that he was going to be helping Kip—he was still clearing the lawn at his home, and they wanted to get it cleaned out before fall. She wondered how anyone could destroy something so grand as the castle that Kip owned now, but then she had a good mother, and Kip had horrific people in his life.

The car that she'd gotten was fun. It was a tiny thing, and she loved driving it. But she was careful too. Lilac had never learned to drive anything until recently, and wondered why she had been so dead set against learning. Sunny sat on her shoulder as they made their way to the two buildings that Griff and her owned.

"The building is empty of all vermin, my lady. I think that once the people and the other things discovered that a dragon was going to be around, they decided to go elsewhere." She told Sunny that it was common for rats and other animals like that to take up residency in an abandoned home, only to have to move on quickly when a dragon showed up. "It's mostly empty but for the basement. There are a few boxes down there that we didn't bother. They are full of papers and such. And some books are in a crate. We have wondered if you'd like to display them in the new shop."

"Yes, if they're old." Sunny assured her that they were very old. "Good, then I'll have someone take them out and clean them up. Maybe see if they can find some dates on them. What else have you found out?"

"The man that is in the forest, he is taking his frustration out on the trees and plants. Just yesterday I had to calm one of the larger trees when James nicked his bark badly. The faeries and I, we repaired it as best we could, but he is still complaining about it." Lilac told her that she'd talk to her mother to see about getting him some extra magic. "That is most helpful. I have someone wanting you to come to his land and ask the waterways to be there for his cattle. Mr. Hartington said that if you help, he will give you some beef. I'm to understand that it is a favorite of dragons, beef."

"We can do that now. Is he aware of what he needs to do if I were to do this for him?" Sunny told her that she'd spoken to him at great length, and that he was also a friend of her mother's. "And she approves of him then?"

"Yes. Lady of the faeries had said that he has been a good

man to them, planting nearly five acres of land full of flowers for them." Lilac turned where she was told to go. "When you help him, my lady, I was wondering if you could have a look at his orchard. The trees are not in the best of shape, and he and his lady wife depend on the sale of the fruits for money in the harder times of winter."

"I can do that."

As they pulled up in front of the large house, she could see that it needed some repairs to it as well. Wondering if there was a committee that did that sort of thing, Lilac decided to talk to the other dragons to see if they could get some men and women together to help the poor in town with this sort of thing.

The elderly man and his wife came out of the house to greet them. "I'm Lilac. I'm to understand that you might need some help with the waterways around here?"

"Yes, miss. We've all but lost all our sheep and cattle because of the damming above us. They told us when they were building that we'd not have any troubles with them. But they took away our source of water, saying that it was theirs to do with as they wanted." He pointed to the large trek of homes that seemed to be just too shiny to be in such a rural area. "The lack of water is killing all the animals that are beyond us. The farm over, it's been up for sale for a while now. No one wants to buy it without any water rights."

"I'll talk to Danburn. I think he might be able to get them to relent on their strangle hold on you." She moved out to the fields that cattle were trying to graze on. There was very little vegetation, and even less water in the stream that ran down the middle of the big field. Lilac reached out to Danburn and the others as she listed what she was seeing. *The men and women here, they're going to be starved by the time winter comes. And it's hurting not just the cattle and such here, but the land as well. My mother said that she's at her wit's end on trying to help the grounds without the water to keep them well.*

If you take care of the waterway, anyway that you wish, I'll go and have a long talk with the owners of the new development. I believe that they're renting the land from me, so if they don't like what I want from them, then they'll be put out. Lilac could hear the anger in Danburn's voice, and almost felt sorry for the men he was going to talk to. *Also, I have asked Rett to put together some teams to go around to the houses. I'll make sure that Mr. Hartington is pushed up to the front. I've known them all my life, and they're good people.*

She sat in the middle of the field, the cows ignoring her for the most part. While they chewed on the dead or dying grasses, she buried her fingers in the dirt and reached out to the waters under her. They were deeper than she'd thought they'd be, having to go that far to make sure that they were safe from the work being done at the housing development.

My lady. I will give you what I have. There is very little, I'm afraid. The houses up yonder, they are sucking us dry daily. Lilac asked him what was going on. *They are filling large holes with our waters, making fountains that waste more than they save when the water splashes along the paths they have made. Watering of the grasses there is fine, but they do it for days on end, and there is little we can supply to other places. There is a rumbling sound that is working very hard to pull what little we have from the earth.*

Lilac followed the source and felt the engine as it worked hard, spraying out odors that were harming the land as well. Digging deeper into the land, she pulled the water from the machine, then moved it with her hands when she had it. Narrowing the water to a pinpoint, stronger than any metal that the machine was made of, Lilac rammed the water into it and shattered its sound. The laughter from the soil made her smile.

131

The water being released wasn't enough. Now she had to open the streams that had laid dormant for so long. Flooding the grass with the water that had all but gone away, she felt it splash over her as the cows with her called out their stress of what was happening. In minutes the water was where it had been for decades, snaking its way through the ground and over rocks as it made its way to ponds and lakes that had been starved.

Sitting where she was for a little while longer, she asked the earth to take the bounty, as there would be no more trouble with the men. Hoping that Danburn would fix this for them, Lilac guided the water to the home of one of the men at the company, and flooded their pool so that it ran over the tops and into their manicured yard. When she stood up, Lilac looked around and saw that one of the other creatures of the earth had given the grounds a boost. The trees were uncurling leaves that had been long since gone. Flowers and grass sprang up in places where the water had not been for longer than the seedlings could remember.

Lilac saw her mom then, the faeries with her working to plant flowers and seeds that they'd had for such a time as this. Walking back to Mr. Hartington, she could see the happiness on his face, and was glad to see that he wasn't wasting any time in getting his other plants watered as well.

"Thank you, my lady. I cannot put into words how much we appreciate what you've done for us today." She thanked him for asking for the help. "I almost didn't want to. But my lady wife, she said that no harm could come from asking. I guess she was correct in that. How long do you think it will be before they dam us up again?"

"Never, I hope. Lord English has gone to speak with them about the water. If this company gives you any more trouble, you can contact me or Lord English to have us come back. There is no reason for them to waste what is there for all to use." He nodded and smiled again. "You're a good man, sir. I thank you for your help in this."

"You have my deepest gratitude, my lady. And I'm ever so glad that you've come to be a part of the lair. Lord English and his other dragons, they have taken good care of us over the years. And he will continue to do the same, I would bet." She assured him that he would. "If you ever find yourself wanting a pie or such, my wife makes the best. You just ask anyone. And now that we'll have fruits to use, we'll be able to stock them up for the winter too. Thank you again."

As she made her way back to the car, Danburn contacted her. He was in good humor, she could almost feel it, and when he told her what he'd done, Lilac laughed as well. It seemed that Danburn wasn't satisfied with the reason that the developer had given him about the water, and had ordered him off his land. Danburn now had a great many houses to finish, and he'd do so with the earth in mind.

~*~

Griff looked up when he heard his name being called. He saw his brother coming toward him, and nearly laughed when he seemed to be cursing at him. With both his arms in a sling, he looked like a man that had been beaten to shit and came out on the losing side of it. Griff crossed his arms over his chest and waited on him to get to him. As soon as he was close enough to smell, he backed away from him. A skunk had apparently taken exception to James, and had given him the once over.

"This is all your fault." He asked James how he'd come to that conclusion. "You have everyone out for me. And I don't care for it. Call them off and I might let you live a bit longer. You see, I've finally figured out how to kill you."

133

"And you want me to do something for you when you just admitted that you're going to kill me? You do know that it doesn't make me want to do a damned thing for you when you say shit like that." James looked around, so Griff did as well. "Carmine isn't here, if that's who you're looking for. But if you'd like to tangle with her again, I can get her here right now."

"No, I don't wish for you to call that child. She's going to pay as well, just you wait and see. But what I want you to do is die. You, and that fucking bitch of a so called mate and our mother. Why she ever came back is beyond me. I liked it just fine when I thought her to be dead." Griff told him that he hadn't, and was glad for her being around. "You would. She's nothing. I'm the oldest male, and she should be doing what I want, not whatever flitters through her empty head."

"I don't think that Mom has an empty head either, James. She's very intelligent. She did outsmart you enough to get away from you when she could." Griff laughed, and he could see the boiling anger on his brother. "You should really behave yourself from now on. I have permission to kill you now, and I won't hesitate if it comes to that."

"You can't kill me. Why do I have to keep telling people this? I'm an immortal. I cannot be killed. And as the oldest son, you should be bowing before me instead of arguing with me at every turn. I don't care for it, Griffith. You'll see what angering me does for you." Griff stared at him for a full minute before he threw back his head and laughed. It felt wonderful to find such humor in what his brother was saying. "What, pray, do you find so funny now? You think I'm not going to kill you?"

"You just explained to me that you can't be killed because you're an immortal, right?" James just nodded. "Well, dumbass, I'm an immortal too, and so was Father. In fact, I'd say that

134

you and Father had a great many alike traits, wouldn't you? I mean, neither of you were dragons. You might have both been immortals, but you managed to kill him, correct?"

Griff saw the exact moment that James got it. When he backed away, taking two steps to Griff's one, he watched as every plan his brother had been concocting ran over his face, only to be discarded.

"Stay away from me, Griffith. I swear if you don't, I'll figure out a way to end your life so that I never have to be around you again." Griff told him to go ahead. He'd shoot those plans down as well. "You think you're so smart, don't you? The great dragon Griffith. Well, I have news for you. I have your mate."

He reached out to Lilac and she told him that she was fine. "No, you don't. She's working a field right now, helping a man get his crops in. You never were a good liar, James." Griff backed his brother up to the building across the street from where they'd been. "You're nothing to me, James. Not even worthy of me trying to convince you to try and redeem yourself. I'm going to enjoy ending your life, and when I do, you can bet that we'll have a bigger celebration than we did for my birthday. Did I tell you how much fun it was to be celebrating with friends and family?"

"I'm your fucking family. Your older brother, as a matter of fact. When are you going to pay homage to me? Treat me like the superior being that I am?" Griff pretended to think about it, then told him never. "You will, brother, I promise you that you will."

He stalked away, and for now, Griff let him. The time would come when he'd have to end his life, but he thought that letting him think for a bit longer that he could get the upper hand would make it so much sweeter when Griff did kill him. He figured with all the faeries watching over James, and the broken arms, he'd have a hard time killing anything, much less the unsuspecting townspeople.

There was no love left for James. Anything that he might have felt for him had long since dried up. James had turned everyone that knew him against him from the moment he killed the first woman. And then when he'd killed his father, Griffith had decided that he had no use for him and nothing kind left to feel for him.

Making his way back to the building that he was in, Griff thought of all the times as children that James had spoiled things for him. Like the first girlfriend that he'd had. James had hurt her, saying that he was Griffith. He'd never gotten over how he'd pulled that one off. Of course, he'd only been about ten or so, but it still hurt him to this day.

Then there were the trips they'd had as a family. The times when James would come into his room while he was gone and break his things that he had collected. Every little thing that Griff had, James would spoil it. But Griff hadn't given up on his brother, trying hard every day to make him a part of what he was doing. Until he decided it wasn't worth his time to try any more.

"Like that did me any good." Realizing that he was talking to himself, Griff laughed. The building was empty and echoed along the walls like there was a large speaker at each end.

The building he was in needed to be torn down. What he was looking for in it when James had shown up was if there was anything salvageable in it. So far, he'd found some old oak floors that could be repurposed, as well as some old doorknobs and light fixtures. As he was marking the things that he wanted to preserve, he heard someone calling his name from below him. He told Lilac where he was.

"I've been helping with the waterway outside of town."

She told him what she'd done and what Danburn had done as well. "He said that he'd take care that the houses were finished and then sell them off with the land they were on. I guess Danburn owns a lot of land around the world, and has to try and remember it or go to Noah. Did you know that Noah has been with him for longer than anyone else?"

"I know. When Danburn and Kendrick have a son, Noah will move to be his butler. Danburn will have someone else, someone that has been trained by Noah. But for now, he'll watch over the baby. By the way, did you hear what they named her?" Lilac said that she had and smiled. "Yes, I knew that you'd hear about it before me."

The little girl had a mouthful of a name. She was Princess Elissa, Lady of the Castle English, Lady Hannah Prince Royal of the Realm. Titles for dragons weren't that much different than for others, but enough so that you knew who was on the grand scale of things. Also, Lady Hannah, what she would go by when it was a casual gathering, would be second to the throne until there was a son born to her parents. Then she would be third in line. Griff had a feeling that she'd run the castle and the realm as well as her father was, and as good as any sibling that she had too.

"I was thinking about something." He paused in what he was doing to give her his full attention. "I was thinking that we should make it official. I'd like for you to marry me. Soon."

"All right. Do I get any say in this, or do you have it all planned out?" He laughed when she blushed. "I would love to marry you, my dear. And soon sounds good to me as well."

"Your mom is making the arrangements now. She asked me what sort of wedding I wanted, then just told me that small was not what she wanted for her favorite son. I guess it'll be large no matter what I say." Griff told her that she could count on it. "I thought you'd say that. And as soon as this shit is over with James, I want to go on a long trip, just the two of us, and have a nice honeymoon. In places that I can make you whimper like a little baby while I make you my sex bitch."

He laughed. Griff hugged Lilac to him and told her how much he loved her. Having this woman in his life, it was going to be a rollercoaster ride all the time, he just knew it. And frankly, he didn't care so long as they were together. After telling her that she had to help him, they sorted out the things that were in the building in a short time and went to dinner. He thought that this could be the best time in his life, just having the two women in his life that he loved more than he did himself.

Chapter 10

This was it. The plan of all plans. James was quite proud of himself. He'd not only been able to devise a plan that was epic, but it would take out all the people that he hated most in the world. And—and this was the best part—he'd have all the gems and jewels that he wanted. Just before he killed them, James was going to make them beg, like he'd wanted his father to do—but this would be a major payoff. These were going to be dragons sobbing and begging for their lives.

He'd found some notes that he'd completely forgotten about in the cave that disproved everything that his brother had told him. There was a way to kill a dragon, and it was quick and immediate. You only had to take off their heads, just like normal people, and that would end their lives. Of course, it would his as well if they were to do that to him, but that just wasn't going to happen. Not to him. Giddy with glee at finding a way to end this shit, he danced around the campfire that he'd started.

He had no food to cook over the hot flames, however. The grocery store that he'd been hitting up on a daily basis had called the police on him when they'd caught him with several steaks and some other foods. Christ, he'd only just barely gotten away without the food when they arrived to take him in. James was sure that Griffith or his mother had had something to do with that. The man at the store had a list of things that he'd been taking, and he wanted money for it all. Money that James just did not have.

"I swear, it's like they know my every move." He had an idea that they did. The ground had spies in it. The bugs and shit flying around would have been telling on him. He knew that there were creatures of the earth around all the time. Not only had he seen them, but his parents had made sure that he knew about them so that he'd never cause them harm. "Like that wasn't just an invite for me to terrorize them. I did it just to spite you all."

His parents had even had them in his house, doing odd jobs and such. They'd had their own gardens too, just for the faeries and brownies. To him it seemed a total waste of time. And money. The flowers did no one any good other than the stupid bugs. Christ, his parents had been ignorant.

He was as healed as he thought he was going to be now. James still had trouble with his hands on occasion, and his arms would kink up when the weather was wet. He hated the early mornings most of all. When the dew was around, it was like an invitation to cause him a great deal of pain. James was going to make them all pay for that too. Especially that little brat.

He had figured out how she'd hurt him—or how she'd not hurt him. There wasn't a scent of magic anywhere close to her. And she'd been acting all powerful. But now that he was away from her, he had reasoned that she was only the front man—the real magic had come from one of the others.

"How stupid do they think I am? You'd have to get up very

140

early in the morning to pull one over on me." Something else that he'd been doing was practicing his name. When Griffith was gone, he'd inherit all his titles. Not to mention wealth as well. "I'll have it all."

Putting out his fire, he went to the nearby creek to wash up. He had a new shirt on, one that he'd managed to keep under his shirt when he'd been run off. James wanted them to sit up and take notice of him today, just before he killed them.

Leaning over the water, he reached his hand into it and felt something hit him in the back of the head. Looking around as he sat in the stream, he could see no one, and nothing that would have fallen on him. Standing up, he felt the water rush over his legs and he was down again. Christ.

"What the fuck is going on here?" Of course no one answered him, so he tentatively tried to stand again. Whoosh, the water seemed to tangle around his feet, and this time he went into the water head first. Coming up out of the stream this time, he heard laughter. Sitting on the bank was none other than his woman.

"Hello, dumbass. Are you enjoying your bath? You seem to be having some trouble there." He asked her what she was doing here. "I've come to warn you off. Not that I think it will do me much good, but that's the reason. And to have some fun with you."

Before he could guess what she was talking about, he was being lifted by the water, by the fucking water, and held there. There was nothing that he could hold onto, as the water was as slippery as glass. James stared at her as she leaned back on her hands and smiled at him.

"I suppose you think that I'm to be afraid of this. I'm not. It's not very nice that someone is playing tricks on me so early in the morning." She asked him if he really thought that. "Of course. Trickery will get you nowhere. What is your name, anyway? The last time I had you, I neglected to ask you that."

"No, you didn't care, that's why you never knew it. And I have no intention of telling you now either. Let's just call me, Wife to Your Brother." He cursed at her, and she smiled bigger. "Does your mother know that you curse like that? Who, by the way, is a very nice person. Why would you want to murder her? I mean, it's not like she's done anything wrong to you."

"She was in the way." The woman nodded as if she understood him. "Are you trying to make me think that you understand the workings of my mind? No one can do that. I'm way beyond any intelligence that you might think you have. I'm much older than you as well. Which also makes me stronger than you are."

"So, you think that you're the one controlling the water? And I'm incredibly older than you, moron." The water started tossing him into the air and catching him. It was dizzying. Up and down, swirling around like a top. When he finally settled again, he had to hold his belly, or he'd be sick all over himself. "I'm the holder of water. A faerie of considerable age. And in turn, your wonderful loving brother, the total opposite of you, is my king."

"Griffith is no more king than I am. And you? What do you hope to gain by telling such lies?" He was lifted once more, this time to a height that he knew if he was dropped, he was going to hurt again. "Put me down. Right now."

He should have chosen his words better, because as soon as he said now, the water disappeared from under him and he plummeted to the earth. The water, he thought, was as hard if not harder than the ground when he hit it.

Every part of him hurt again. Not only his arms and wrists, but his legs and his head. Getting out of the water, he noticed that he was covered in blood. Finding the huge knot on his head, he glared at the woman.

"You bitch. Look what you did." She asked him if he was ready to admit that she had power over the water. "No. But I'm sure that you think you do. Whatever happened there, you can bet that I could do it better. Not because you're a woman, but because I'm so much better than you."

Something grabbed him around the waist and he felt himself being dragged back to the water. Trying to pull it off, his hands only met with water, and as it tightened its grip on him, James was afraid. If she did indeed have control over the water, she could hurt him badly with it.

This time instead of taking him up high and dropping him, he was held up by his leg and dipped over and over into the water like a damned tea bag. Every time he'd come up sputtering like a fool, James could hear her laughing. The bitch was going to pay for this. Dropped again, this time on the shore, he laid there for several minutes trying to catch his breath. He was coughing up water, and his nose was leaking it out too.

James closed his eyes, hoping that she was tired of this game and would leave him alone. Making a mental note to hurt her for this, he let his body go limp with exhaustion.

When he woke, he was stiffer than he'd ever been. His clothing was still damp, and that had not helped his aching body. Moving to where he'd been cooking his meals, he found that his matches were now wet, and the wood that he'd had to drag to the site was wet too. Looking around, he realized that it had rained. A great deal, by the looks of things.

Making his way to find some drier wood and a way to light the shit when he got it, he noticed that anything about ten feet from where he was camping was dry. James did a complete circle around the campsite and saw that he was right. It had rained, or whatever, just in the circle around his area.

"You fucking bitch. You're going to pay for this." He raised his fists to the air and screamed at her again. "What the fuck is wrong with you that you'd do this to me? What the hell have I done to you yet? Nothing. Nothing at all, because someone let you go. Now, you'll pay. All of you will."

Dragging the dry wood to the fire pit that he had, James stopped long enough to curse them out, tell them what he had plans for, as well as how much he was going to make them suffer. It took him longer because of that, too.

Once he had all the wood he thought he'd need, he started trying to figure out how to get a fire going. He remembered once that someone on the television had rubbed two sticks together and that seemed to work. So, James set about doing that.

"If I was a fucking dragon like I should have been, then this would be easier." He screamed and fell back when the fire started in a huge ball of flames. When a shadow fell across him, he looked up at his brother. "What the fuck are you doing here? You're supposed to wait for me to come to you. Damn it, Griffith, don't you understand protocol?"

"Yes, well, I didn't think that we had to stand on ceremony when one of us was living off the land. And you're welcome, by the way. I don't want you to freeze to death before I have a chance to talk to you." Griffith sat down, again uninvited. "I heard you had a nice morning with my wife. Did she get you nice and clean?"

He was making fun of him, and James hated him even more. Instead of telling him off, like he wanted to do, he put more wood onto his fire. The insolent bastard was going to get his. James was going to make sure of it.

"What is it you want? If it's to make fun of me more, you can just be on your way. I have things to do." Griffith didn't

144

move from his spot. "Did you not hear what I just said to you? Go the fuck away."

"I will when I'm ready." The hardness of Griffith's voice made him cringe back from him. "Now, I'd like to ask you to give yourself in to the council and be done with this plotting and planning. You're not going to be able to kill any of us. First of all, to remove our heads, as you have planned, you need a sword. And I just don't see one. Unless of course you have it hidden away. But I don't think so. The mother of the earth would have told me."

"Mother of the earth? Are you drunk? High? Fuck you. I will succeed, and there won't be a thing you can do about it." Griffith nodded and picked up a stick, and played in his fire with it. "You don't have my permission to bother my things. Go away and leave me in peace. Or die. That would just make my day to see you dead."

"Yes, I'm sure that it would. But, since I gave you this flame, you had better be nice to me or I'll take it back. Or I'll have my mate come and dunk you a few more times in the water. Now shut up and listen to me." Again, his voice was hard, and James felt as if he had no choice in the matter but to shut up and listen. "You have twenty-four hours to turn yourself in. If you do not, I will kill you. Not maim you, not hurt you a little, but remove your empty head from your shoulders as you did to our father."

"He was weak, did you know that? Begged me over and over to let him go. To come for you instead of him. But I had him where I wanted him, and I killed him. My plan was to kill both you and Mother too, but I was thwarted in that. But I'm ready for you now. And I'm going to be the one removing heads, not you." Griffith laughed; it was loud, and seemed to come from the entire forest the way it echoed around the two of them. "You think this is funny, Griffith?"

"I do, as a matter of fact. You can't even build a decent fire, and you expect me to be quaking in my boots? Not hardly. I'm a much bigger man than you would ever be." Griffith stood up, and James felt his balls tighten to his body when his brother went from man to dragon in a breath. *You'll heed my warning, James, or this will be the last thing you ever see. I promise you that.*

His dragon was enormous, much larger than he'd remembered. And the helmet across his head was dangerous looking, like he could lower his head and ram the barbs there into a person. Suddenly his wings spread out from his body, large and gleaming, like gems and jewels were all over it. Just as he was reaching out to touch them, to see if they were as soft as they looked, they flapped once and raised Griffith off the ground. Then with that, he disappeared into the sky.

James stayed where he was, only moving when the fire started to die down. His brother was a dragon. A fucking dragon. And he was going to try and kill him with it.

He knew that his brother was a dragon, had seen him in all his glory when they'd been kids growing up. Every time he'd seen his brother flying with his friends, James had thought him smaller than the others, and had had a good laugh at the inadequateness of him. Now he thought that Griffith was even bigger than Damn Bird. Fuck, this was getting out of hand.

"I need a better plan." Sure he did, he thought. One that wouldn't have him roasting on a spit by his own brother. "I'll work on it, and they'll rue the day that they threatened me. See if they don't."

~*~

Griff loved what he was doing with Lilac today. The auction that they were attending had all the things that he wanted for his home, and a great deal of them for the museum. He knew the man that was selling his things—he'd been a friend of his

146

for quite a number of years. Carson was a warlock of good standing. Retiring from life, he'd decided to let go of a lot of his things.

"I leave you alone for ten or so years, and what do you do? Go and find you a love and become a king of the water." They hugged as only good friends could do. "You have a lovely mate, my friend. She's eyeing my collection of gems. I have told her that whatever she wants, she could have, but she is telling me that she's going to buy them and not have them given to her. Does she realize that I don't need the money any more than you do?"

"I'm sure that she does." They both watched her standing over the boxes while the auctioneer tried to get a much higher bid on some of them. "She won't go over what she is willing to pay for things. Me? I will get all caught up in the sale and the magic of it, and usually spend too much. But Christ, it's fun."

When she got her boxes, she danced around for a minute before collecting them. Adding them to her growing pile, Griff followed Carson into his home. The house along with the property wasn't up for auction or sale. Carson said that he might return someday, and wanted a place to live.

"I've decided that I want you and the missus to have the house." Griff started to tell him no when he held up his hand. "Treasure abounds in here. The sublevels, well below the basement, has my lab, as well as an extensive collection of wines. I don't know anyone I trust more than you to take care of this place."

"I thought you were planning to return someday." Carson said that he was just too tired. "Once you rest up, you'll find that you want to come back."

"I'm sure if that were true, you'd allow me to stay here until I got bored with life again." Griff told him of course he would.

"I miss my Mae. She was my heart and soul. Kept me alive; not just kept my heart beating, but just kept me from becoming an ass, or someone that could turn to the other side of this magic."

"I'm so sorry about that, Carson. Until I met my own mate, I couldn't have understood what you mean. You have my heartfelt sympathy. I don't know what I'd do if I were in the same place." Carson hugged him again and they sat on the only two pieces of furniture in the living room. "I'll help you out by keeping an eye on the place for you, but I won't take it. When you've had enough rest, come back and we'll have a nice steak dinner together."

Carson nodded and smiled at him. In that moment, Griff knew that the man wasn't going to come back. Nor was he only going to rest. Carson was going to end his own life, and there would be no talking him out of it.

They talked for a bit longer, nothing really earth shattering, before they made their way outside again. Griff had to laugh. Lilac's pile had grown exponentially, and she was carrying two more items to her pile even as they made their way to her.

"You would not believe what I got all this for. And I know what you're going to say — we don't need another wine opener, we have four. Nor do we need any more pots and pans. But I have a plan." He asked her what that was, not caring one bit how much she spent or on what since she was having such a good time. "Carson, you should have a talk with that auctioneer. He's just giving it all away."

"You enjoy it, my dear. I'm glad that someone that appreciates a good deal is getting it." She told them that she was going to set up a storage area with these things to give to people in need. "I love that idea. Very much so. Had I thought of it, I would have just donated this all to you and your cause. But I would have missed seeing you having such a wonderful time in getting them."

"I do like a good deal."

They both laughed, and Lilac said she was going back to the auction. Griff loved this woman more than he could put to words. He looked at Carson when he laughed.

"I do believe your lovely mate has you all twisted up and wrapped with a pretty bow." Griff didn't even try and deny it; he said that she had him hook, line, and sinker. "It shows. You're happy, and that's such a good thing for you."

"It is. I wish that I could say the same for you." Carson told him that the two of them had given him such joy today. "You're a good friend, Carson, the best. I'm going to miss you."

"And I you. To change the subject, I heard that your mother is alive. And that James is causing heartache in your town." Griff told him about Lilac being caught by him, as well as how he'd been pissed about Mom being alive. "Yes, I can see that about him. What a monster, if you don't mind me being honest with you."

"No, I agree with you. Even Mom has washed her hands of him." Carson said that he thought that was a good idea too. "You know that James killed our father. He beheaded him because, as far as I can tell, he wouldn't hand over the castle to James and any money there might have been."

"The council, I'm assuming, thinks they can't do anything because he's not a dragon." Griff told him that was pretty much it. "Danburn, he can make a case for you. He did attempt to kill your mother, correct?"

"That's what he did tell them. So, I've been given permission to end his life. Any of us can, I guess. But Mom doesn't want me to do it. She thinks that it'll haunt me." Griff laughed—it was bitter. "Like what he's done so far doesn't haunt me already."

When Lilac joined them, he held her to his lap. She was a

149

balm to him, giving him the security that he'd not realized that he needed. When Carson moved away, the auctioneer needing him, Griff asked her what she'd gotten so far.

"Quilts. Three of them that I'd like to put on the beds at home after I get them cleaned. And there were some pretty vases that I got, handmade I think, that will go in the nearly finished bedroom." He told her that he loved her. "And I love you. Tell me what's wrong, Griff. Whatever it is, I'm sure that the two of us can solve it."

"Nothing really. I was just talking to Carson, and he asked me about James. I think Carson's going to ask to have his life ended. That saddens me too. I know how I would feel if something were to happen to you. That's why he is selling all this off and has given us his home and the contents." She whistled and he nodded. "I know. It's a big ranch, and there are bottles of expensive wines in the cellar."

"He's a very nice man." Griff told her that he had been one of his best friends for a long time. "If he's going to go through with this, tell him to let me know where his mate is and I'll have the faeries make a garden over them both. That way, others who feel as you do about him can go and talk to him."

"That's very nice, love. Thank you for that." She nodded and asked him if he was ready for round two. "More? Are you going to put us in the poor house?"

"See all my stuff over there? I've only spent thirty-four dollars. That's all for all the boxes. I'm telling you, Griff, they're selling his things for too cheap. I'm not complaining—I've gotten some amazing deals—but Carson might want to check into this." He told her that like them, Carson had more than enough money. "I figured. But still. Anyway, come on, I want to bid on the two cabinets in the other ring. One of them is very old and would look good as a credenza in the hallway."

He looked around for Carson as Lilac waited on what she wanted. Griff saw him near the stack that Lilac had put aside and saw him put a large bag of something with them. He'd bet anything that it was his gems. When he waved at him, Griff had a feeling that he'd never see him again, and relayed the message from Lilac to him.

Tell her that would be perfect. Mae is out by the tree that I found her at. Napping like a beautiful faerie. Yes, that would be wonderful. You thank her for me. And tell her that this gift is just for her for being your mate. Take care of her, my friend. She's well worth it. He agreed with him. *Goodbye, Griffith Alexander Farley, the Fourth Earl of Alexander's Folly. The Duke of Winebarger and Baron of Windemere Castle. I shall miss you more than any other.*

And I you, my friend. Forever and a day, I will miss you.

Then he was gone—just disappeared in the air. Griff did wonder if the auctioneer knew the power he was selling for and decided that he didn't care. Carson would make this good for him, even though things were going so cheaply.

They managed to fill the back of the cargo carrier that they'd gotten, in addition to putting some breakable things in the bed of the new truck, which was very nice. Griff thought they'd been better prepared for this trip for auction hunting. Lilac had brought some old quilts and some extra cardboard to put between things like plates.

After they were loaded up, they made their way to the hotel they were staying in that night. They'd order a pizza in, as they had been doing for these trips. Both of them fell asleep even before they'd finished off the pizza. Auctioning was hard work, he thought with a laugh just as he was dozing off, after checking the door locks again and covering up Lilac.

151

Chapter 11

With no hope of getting into the castle to get anything to use to cut their heads from their bodies, James made his way to town. The plan had been revised, and he was going to tell them, whoever would listen, that he needed to have a better place to stay. Even a hotel would be good, he'd tell them. Then he'd use the money that they'd surely throw at him—for being the poor, hurt brother of Griffith—for bribing one of the idiots at the castle to let him come in and take one of the many swords that he knew were there.

"Mother dear, you just saved my ass and didn't know it." He'd seen them being taken in when his mother had moved into the castle. She'd been making a big show of being there too. Once she'd had a line of people coming in for some sort of tea party. He knew this because all the bitches that went in were wearing big fluffy hats and had on white gloves. "Why would you wear gloves to eat? Women are stupid, that's all I can say about that."

He saw the staff going into the house at about six in the morning. Christ, he'd spent another nasty night out in the cold

153

and wet, only to almost miss them when he'd gone to take a piss behind a tree. Going as close to the house as he could without going to the barrier, he called out to one of the workers that he recognized. James wasn't sure what his name was or what job he had at the castle, but knew that he'd seen him hanging around.

"Hey, buddy." The guy looked like he was going to ignore him, so James threw a rock at him, hitting him in the head. "When I call for you, dumbass, you answer. I want you to get me in the castle, now."

"No." He turned his back on him and James threw another rock at him, this time missing him by a mile. "You're not going to get anyone here to let you in, no matter how many rocks you throw. Go away."

"I want you to just allow me to get in and get one of the swords that my father promised me. It would go a long way to letting me eat a decent meal." The guy just stared at him. "I'll come back tonight and give you money. I don't know how much yet—I have to get it from Griffith. He...he owes me a lot of money."

"He does, does he? I'm sure that he has more than enough to not have to borrow it from you, if you had anything to lend." When he turned his back again, James was ready to leap through the magic to kill the man, but he paused and turned back again. "Your father was a good man. A good master, and a better man than you could ever hope to be. His son, Griffith, is a great deal like him. And we all know for a fact that you murdered the lord of this castle, right there in that very forest. Stay away, Jiminy Cricket, or I'll go to Lord Griffith and tell him what you want."

"Get back here, dammit. So what if I killed my father? We've—Griffith and I, we've patched things up." The man laughed and headed back to the castle. By the time James could think of a nasty reply, the man and all the other workers were gone. "Mother shit balls, I hate people."

Stomping toward town, James tried to get all his anger out before he met up with his brother. He wanted to make sure that he looked sincere when he asked him for money. Also, he hoped that he'd just fork over an invite to the castle again. It had been a few days since he'd hurt anyone. He could tell him that he was turning over a new leaf. James laughed. Like that was ever going to happen.

It took him all day to make it to his brother's house. The fact that he lived way on the other side of town from where he'd grown up was just ignorant on his part. Why did he even have a home? The castle was right there. But he supposed that if he did live in the castle, he'd have been harder to get to. As it was now, walking all day and well into the night to get to him was hard enough.

James found him a place to take a nap while he waited for the sun to come up. He figured that everyone would be in their nice, cozy beds with the air conditioning running, while he suffered through the heat and had to sleep on a slab of concrete. Grumbling about how he was starving and sore got him no answers, but he'd have plenty of them tomorrow, just as soon as he found one of the many jerk-offs that were around. He knew that the others would tumble once he killed Griffith.

Sleep was fitful for him. When he woke the sun was just cresting over the mountain behind Damn Bird's house, and he could see that someone had been up before him and was mowing the lawns at a few of the larger homes. Griffith would have someone doing that for him. He was too lazy to do it himself.

"I, however, am not lazy, but know that I have servants to do the grunt work. Why else would you pay someone to be

155

at your home unless to make them work for you?" Getting up slowly, feeling every bit his age lately, he walked to the house and waited at the gate. "Keeping his own brother out. What sort of person does that?"

Of course, he would when he owned the castle again. And he'd only hire people that had worked for the rest of them. James figured they'd be happy to have a job when he was finished, and he was going to hire them for half pay. That would teach them to work for a traitor like Griffith. And the rest of them, including Damn Bird.

When Griffith came out of his house, it gave James a fright. His brother came right toward him, no hesitation on his part, and it sort of unnerved him a little. Once they were standing as close as he could get to him, Griffith just stared at him. Well, he'd not be the first one to speak in this game of wits. But when Griffith shrugged and walked away, James called him back.

"Why do you always have to win? Christ, you're a pain in my ass. I want you to give me money. I've been being a good citizen, and you need to—"

"No. If there is nothing else, I want to have breakfast with my wife." James called him every name that he could think of. "Yes, that shows me just how much of a good citizen you are. What do you want, James? I'm not going to give it to you, but you might as well have your say. You did walk a long way here for it."

"As I said, I want money. I haven't had a shower in days other than getting drenched in the water and the rain. I'm starving to death, as all the game around me seems to have disappeared. I'm assuming you had something to do with that." Griffith told him that he had. "Why? What have I ever done to you that you'd make your own brother, your older brother, starve?"

"You killed my father." He asked him why he was forever bringing that up. "Because you did it. And I will never forgive you for it. I'm not going to give you money. You're on your own. Deal with it."

"I'm going to enjoy killing you, Griffith. And when you're all dead, I'm going to live in the castle and make it my own. I might even fuck your wife before I take her head off too. What do you think of that?" Griffith said nothing, but he did smile. "You don't believe me, do you? Well, I've a spy in the castle, and they're going to get me whatever I want."

"Sure you do. This spy you have, is it the same man you pelted with rocks just yesterday? If so, then he already told me that you wanted to bribe him to let you in. Of course, he turned you down. You, of all people, wouldn't understand loyalty. And that's what the staff there is, very loyal to me and the family." James screamed at him that he was his family. "No, not anymore. Not since you drew a sword against our father and murdered him for no other reason than you could. Even the one you gave us when you bragged about it hasn't come true, has it? You're no closer to living in the castle than you are to me being your friend. It's just not going to happen."

"You bastard. I fucking hate you." Again, his brother shrugged at him and turned away. James was getting sick of people dismissing him this way. Reaching for him, meaning to teach him a lesson, he watched in horror as Griffith shifted to his great beast. "No, don't hurt me."

The dragon blew heat all around him—never touching him with it, not even getting close enough that it made him too hot. And when Griffith laughed, his dragon making the nastiest noise he'd ever heard, James wanted to hit him, but didn't. He wasn't that stupid. The dragon, he knew, wouldn't stop short of him this time.

157

"Come here again, for any reason, and I will not stop at just scorching the earth around you. I will enjoy taking your life with my dragon. As I have said to you before, and I mean it even more this time, I am going to be the last thing you see before you're dead." The flame surrounded him again, this time coming close enough that he feared for his life. "Go away, James. Or so help me, you'll not live another day."

He left him there, wondering what the neighbors would say about the dragon in the yard. But then James remembered that they were all fucking dragons, including his own dip shit mother. James wanted one thing to go his way. Just one fucking thing. But it seemed that if he was going to get this done, killing off the dragons, he was going to have to come up with something else. Then he saw his mother walking along the street ahead of him.

"Hello, Mother."

She turned and looked at him, and he pulled out the butcher knife that he'd stolen several days ago. It wasn't all that sharp, certainly nowhere near enough to remove her head, but it would get him into the castle, and that was what he needed.

Grabbing her from behind, he put the knife to her throat and held it there. He half guided and half dragged her to the alley. It was the best thing he'd had happen to him since he'd killed his own father. He wondered briefly why she'd not shifted into her dragon, but he figured that she didn't want him hurt. James was her oldest son, after all.

"This will get you nothing, James. Not one penny. Not into the castle, nor will it give you a chance to live out a nice life." He told her to shut up. "What is it you think to accomplish by doing this?"

"Everything, Mother dear. Everything that I have ever wanted, you're going to be the reason I get it. Call to Griffith.

I know that you can. Tell him that I've got you and that we're headed to the castle."

She said that she'd not do it. He cut into her throat. Seeing the blood there made him hard and excited.

"All right, he's coming."

Getting her to the castle was trickier than he'd thought it would be. First of all, it was all the way across town. Secondly, she wasn't exactly cooperating. So he told his mother to tell him to meet him here, behind the drug store. When she closed her eyes, he figured that she was doing as he asked and laughed. Christ, this was easier than he'd thought it would have been.

The wait wasn't that long, but it wasn't Griffith that showed up, but his woman. James, spittle dripping from his mouth from all the excitement, asked her where Griffith was. He cut a little deeper into his mother's throat just to show her that he wasn't joking around.

"He's coming and is bringing help. Not that they're going to kill you instead of him, but he might need someone there in the event you're stupider than we all know you are already." When she laughed, he wanted to drop his mother and run her through. But he needed Griffith dead first. "Are you, James? Stupid enough to think that you're going to succeed at this?"

"I will, you fucking cunt." She laughed, and he felt his temper take him more. "You just wait. As soon as this business is done with my brother, I'm going to tie you to my bed, in the castle, and fuck you until you're dead."

"You have a little dick, James. I doubt very much that you could fuck anyone to death. Your brother, however, he's really —" Mother cleared her throat and the woman laughed again. "I am sorry, Marissa, I forgot there were decent people around."

"Do try not to talk about sex in front of me, dear. It's more

159

than I want to know about my son." They both laughed, and he cut his mother deeper, feeling the blood rush over his hand as he did so. "I'm thinking that this will be the end of things as I know it, don't you?"

"You're fucking right it's almost the end of you." Mother told him she meant that he'd be dead. "No. I don't think so. You see, I have all the cards, and I'm going to come out of this a rich and happy man."

"If you say so, James." He felt the ground rumble and shift. Looking out at the field behind the store, he saw them all. Eight beautiful dragons. Some he knew, others he had no idea where they'd come from. But Christ, they were a sight to behold. "There they are now. I do hope this will be over soon, I have a hair appointment."

~*~

Griffith stayed as his dragon as he made his way to his brother. They could smell the blood, he and his dragon, and it made them both roar. Calming his other half, his dragon, he told him that this was just what they needed. For James to have made a mistake this large.

But he is harming our mother. Griffith knew that his dragon was indeed the son of his mother too. They were a pair. Dragon to man. *I wish him dead.*

As do I, but we must be careful. Our mate, she has this well under control. And we trust her. If things go the wrong way, we'll be here to kill James. Dragon agreed, but didn't seem all that happy with the outcome. *You trust me, don't you?*

I trust you, yes. And our mate. But I still worry. It is a good solid plan, but nothing ever goes as you wish when dealing with a madman. Lilac moved to stand in front of them in all her grandeur as her natural self. *She is magnificent, is she not?*

Yes. I'm going to ask Noah to paint us together as she is now.

160

Sitting upon your hand. The dragon agreed it would be a sight to behold. *Just let us get this finished, and we'll talk to him about it. I want James finished.*

"Well fucktard, what is it you wanted to see your brother about? If you let Marissa go now, I will guarantee you a swift death." James asked her what she was talking about. "You. Dead. Isn't that what you called them here for? To kill you off?"

"No. He's going to be dead, all of you are. Including Damn Bird." Lilac turned and looked at Griff. Her wink made both he and his dragon feel so much better. "What are you doing all the talking for? I want to have this conversation with someone that has a bit of intelligence."

"You're talking to someone much smarter than you are, moron. I used my time being around forever to have a great education. And even if I hadn't, you have to admit calling dragons to you, while you hold one of their mothers, is about as stupid as it can get. What did you hope to gain by making this monumental mistake?"

"I want you all dead." She laughed, and so did Dragon. "I want to talk to Griffith, not you. Griffith? Are you too afraid to face me?"

He shifted to become a man in that moment. "Nay, I am not afraid of you at all, James. Lilac is here to bargain with you. And failing that, the council has given myself and her permission to end your life. So that we may go on with our own."

"You can't be serious. Why does the dragon council have anything to do with this in the first place?" He told him that he'd killed a dragon. "Mother fuck, Griffith. How many times are you going to bring that up? It's done. It's over. Get over it."

"No, I don't think so. And I will be happy to have you dead and out of our lives. You will be too, James. Surely you can see that you're not going to live." The blood running down his

161

mother's throat had Griff's dragon rushing over him, as if he were going to take him to save their mother. "Let her go, James. Let Mother go."

"No. She's going to get me what I want, and that's you dead. Fuck you and the rest of them. And once I'm in the castle, I'm going to kill you all." He looked at the dragons around them. They were lounging on the grass. Kip was having a good time playing with the faeries that had come to help should they need them. "Allow me entrance to the castle, Griffith, and I'll let her go."

"Done." He could see by the look on James's face that he'd not expected him to give that to him. "You may enter the castle. Call it your own if you wish. But, brother dear, you have to make it there, and I don't see that being an easy task for you."

"Then I'll take her head now." Griffith felt his dragon—he was pissed, and when he consumed him, he knew that he was going to kill James. And if he did, then Mom was going to be hurt as well. "You can't hurt me, Griffith. If you so much as draw in a breath to burn me, I'll cut her head off before you could even get to that point."

I'm a dragon, son. He looked at his mother when she spoke to him through their link. *Griff, I'm a dragon. Your brother is not. End this. I know that I did not wish for you to be the one, but I'm a dragon. Kill him.*

You'll be hurt. I cannot do that to you. She smiled, and he heard her gentle laughter. *I don't find anything about this to be humorous, Mom.*

Hurt is so much better than dead, don't you think? I do, even if you don't. Kill him. Let us all get on with our lives — kill him. He looked at the others; they were all on alert now. *I love you, Griffith, with all that I am. But he will harm you all should he get away with this.*

Before he could summon the breath to breathe over his

mom and brother, the faeries that had been with Kip suddenly materialized in front of him. Before he could figure out what they were about, they attacked, as one, his brother.

The screaming from James would haunt him forever, he thought. The way that the faeries went after him, digging and cutting into his flesh, had his dragon curl around him. Griff wasn't sure if he was protecting him or just giving him comfort, but he watched in horrific detail as his brother was literally dismantled as a person.

Great slices of James's skin were removed. Holes were burrowed into the places where his eyes had been. His fingers were torn off and his clothing stripped away, showing more of how they were cutting him apart. Mom moved away, his hold on her no longer there. And when she stood beside Lilac, Dragon held him tighter, telling him that the faeries had this.

Even torn apart as he was, James still screamed. They had yet to remove his head from his torso, and the rest of him, arms and legs, even his ears, were still intact. Griff wondered why they were toying with him, seemed to be dragging out his death for too long, when Danburn spoke to him.

They cannot kill a creature such as him. The faeries can maim him, incapacitate him, but they cannot take his life. Not remove his head in this. Griff asked him why not. *Because it is the law. Even with him stripped of everything that he was—his titles, money, and castle—he is still a royal. And that makes it so that their hands are tied in this.*

And they were careful of not killing him. He was sure that they could, easily, but they were never close to his neck at any time. That, however, left a great deal of him to suffer. And Griff could see that he was. Suffering as much as anyone he'd ever seen.

"Kill him, Griff." He looked at his mom. "End his suffering.

163

He has paid for what he has done. End his life now."

Nodding once, he saw that the faeries seemed to understand and moved to be beside his mother and Lilac. He briefly wondered if Lilac had commanded them to do this, taking the threat away from his mom. Taking the step necessary to be closer to James, his brother's lips, torn and bleeding, moved. That was when he noticed that the faeries had only removed one of his eyes — the other was staring at him as he lay there bleeding.

You fucked me over. He told James that he had not, he'd done that on his own. *No, you did this. This is all your fault. And as soon as I'm healed, you'll be dead.*

You are nearly so now, James. There is nothing left of you to think you might live. James told him he was an immortal. *You were. At one time you might have been able to recover from such a thing, but killing our father and trying to kill Mom, you began the process of having your immortality stripped from you.*

No, this is your fault. He didn't bother answering him, but watched him lie there. *I hate you, Griffith. And some day you're going to die at my hand.*

It is you that will be dead in a moment. And yet you still hurl insults at me. Threaten me with the very thing that got you here. Why, James? Why did you not care for us the way we tried to you? James laughed, the sound of it gurgled and wet sounding. *You think it's a joke that I'm going to take your life? I told you once, I'd be the last thing you saw. And here we are to that very point.*

Try and kill me, Griffith. Try it. I will prove to you that I am stronger than you. Being first born, it gave me rights and magic that you'll never have. He laughed again. *You're so dim-witted, Griffith. Thinking that you can murder me. And that is what it would be, because you are this all powerful dragon. Try it and see that I am right.*

164

Goodbye, James. I will not lie to you and tell you that I will miss you. I won't tell you an untruth about how much this hurts me to end your life. You have no one to blame but yourself.

Drawing in a deep breath, feeling the heat of his dragon as he readied himself for this, Griff told his brother once again that he would not live through this.

Griff let his breath go. The white of the flame licked at the building they were beside, and that was what he focused on — the building, not his brother. When the screams stopped, the sound of it echoing around the other buildings, he didn't look at the body of James, but turned and walked away when he knew it to be finished.

He took to the skies, wanting to get away, to clear his mind of what he'd just done. Griff landed atop the mountain, which was as much a part of the earth as it was Danburn's home and laid down. The feelings that he was having, they seemed out of proportion to what he'd just done.

Are you all right? Do you need me? He told Lilac that he was fine but needed a moment or two. *All right. But I'm right here should you need me. And the faeries are cleaning up and making the building whole again.*

Yes, tell them I said thanks. He thought about James. *He is dead, isn't he? He seemed so sure that he was coming back. I wouldn't think he would, but right now, I'm second guessing everything.*

No. He's gone. There is nothing left of him. That was good, he told her. *Yes. Your mother is taking it surprisingly well too. She does have some sadness, but not like you'd think.*

She'll be all right. So will I. But I need a few minutes. She told him that she loved him. *And I you, my dear. Very much so.*

In that moment, he wanted a child. One of his own that he and Lilac could raise to be a good man, one of worth and not full of hate. It would be difficult, especially with the world as it

165

was, but he wanted to have a baby with Lilac. He'd talk to her when he got home. Closing his eyes, knowing that he was safe as his dragon, Griff let complete rest take him.

Chapter 12

Nancy sat in the little hotel and looked around. She'd never been to such a homey place before. Even the cleaning staff, young kids that were just out of high school, were courteous and friendly. They had told her that Griffith was a good man and that he was someone to trust. Nancy didn't know what to think. When the man she was meeting showed up, every part of her wanted to run and hide.

"Miss Shipley?" She said that she was Mrs. but was widowed now. "I'm sorry about that. I've recently had a loss as well. Would you like to talk here or at the diner? I heard that you've been there. The food is good, isn't it?"

"Yes, that's fine. I guess I should tell you why I'm here."

He said that he wanted to know, but that they should sit down and order first. The walk to the diner was made in silence, but she kept an eye on how the others in town reacted to seeing him about. There were lots of hellos. Some only nodded and smiled. Two people told Lord Griffith that they were sorry for his loss. Nancy had heard that there had been a death, but not who it had been.

As soon as they were seated, a waitress that had waited on her before came to the table with a large glass of iced tea for him and lemonade for her. That was all she'd ordered to drink since being here.

"Hello, Griff. I was thinking about you yesterday. There are some old pieces of equipment out on my daddy's farm that I wanted to know if you wanted. It's old as sin, but I think with the right kind of care, people would like to see them. There's an old car and a horse drawn buggy. My momma got herself wed up in that. Well, not the buggy, but that's how she got to the church. You want it?" Lord Griffith smiled and said that he would be out to see it today. "Good. All righty then. You having the special? It's country fried steak and mashed taters, as well as some green beans and a bowl of chicken noodle. You can have a salad if you want it. We made the kind your wife enjoys."

"Yes, I'll have the special." He looked at Nancy and she nodded, telling him that she'd enjoy that as well. When the waitress walked away, he seemed to relax. "She'll talk your arm off, but she's good at what she does. And her mother is about as old as the buggy, I'm thinking. I've been around her on several committee meetings. Now, what can I do for you?"

"I didn't know you were a twin." He said that few did, that his brother wasn't well liked. "Yes, I know that. I've come here— Well, I came here to tell you off. To perhaps hurt you in some way. But I don't think it was you. Actually, I know that it wasn't you who— My sister. Several months ago, she was murdered. Killed by your twin."

"I'm so sorry. You cannot believe how sorry I am that this happened to you. My own wife, she was one of his victims as well." She nodded and then looked away. "You said that you came here to find me. May I ask what led you to believe that you'd find your answers here?"

"He told her his name. Your name. He took her out a couple of times, promising her all sorts of things. I had met him too, just in passing. He— I don't know his real name." He told her he was James. "James. He wasn't particularly nice, not even before she was killed. I told her to stay away, to break it off, but she liked him."

"James was killed several days ago." She said that she'd heard that as well. "I'm so very sorry. We, my family and I, are trying to find all the women that met with him. And we're setting up a fund to help with funeral costs. Some of them, a very few, are alive but not well."

Nancy looked at him. "You're very wealthy." He said that he was. "Yet you met with me, here in your home town, like a regular person."

"I'm not sure what you mean by that. We're all just regular people." Nancy shook her head and told him she didn't mean to insult him. "You didn't. I just wondered what you meant, that's all."

"I'm broke." She laughed, bitterly. "My sister, Belinda Shipley, was all I had in the world. And when she was found— killed, I had to use all my resources to bury her, and then take out a loan to come here to fuck you over."

"I can help you, Nancy." She told him that wasn't necessary. "But it is. My wife would have my head if I were to allow you to have had this expense and not reimburse you in some way."

A beautiful woman came in then and sat down beside her. The man took up most of the other seat, and Nancy assumed this was the wife. It would only figure that a man as good looking as him would have a drop dead gorgeous wife too. Lord Griffith introduced her to his wife.

"Lady Lilac, it's nice to meet you." She said to please just call her Lilac. And then Griffith told her to call him Griff. "You're so very nice, the two of you. I've been holding onto this anger, this pissed off-ness, for so long that it's hard to equate you being related to that monster. I'm sorry."

"Don't be. He was a monster. Of the worse sort. And I'm so sorry that you became one of his prey as well." She said it had been her sister. "No, you both were his prey in this. He hurt whole families with his depravity. And ruined a great many lives in the process. I'm very glad that you came to see us. This way when we start to contact others like you and your sister, we can include you in this. His mother, Marissa, she's the one that is helping us put together what we think families might need."

"I wouldn't even hazard a guess on what people would need to have closure on this. Just knowing that he's dead— I'm sorry Griffith, but knowing that he's dead, it does help a great deal." Griffith said that he agreed with her. "The things that he did to her. The way that—"

Nancy cried, something that she'd sworn that she was finished with. But when Lilac wrapped her up in her arms, it felt as if she could let go. To help herself heal now. Blubbering all the things that came into her head, things that James had done to Belinda, was easier than it had been. Just because these people cared.

When she was cried out, she looked around and there wasn't anyone staring at her. And Griffith had left the two of them there. Feeling embarrassed, she told Lilac that she was sorry. That she'd not meant to make a fool of herself.

"You didn't. You were hurt and holding that in can break you or make you. I think you'll begin to heal now."

Nancy nodded and looked at the plate of food in front of her. "I don't think I can eat now."

"Of course, you can. I'll have Griff's, though I think they know him well enough to double up his meal. There isn't any way that I can eat all this." Another woman joined them, and Nancy was introduced to Marissa, mother to James and Griff. "She was just telling me that she's not hungry. And I have Griff's plate."

"I should hope you hadn't ordered all that. But, my dear, you must eat. Go ahead — now that you've been lifted out of the mess that James put you in, you're going to feel much better." The other woman took a biscuit off the plate of Lilac and started putting butter on it. "I've been looking for someone that could come in a few days a week. I have to admit, I thought it would be a good deal easier than it's turned out to be. I don't suppose you have any skills to keep an old woman straight, do you? Scheduling things for me is a big thing, and someone to keep me sane on other days."

"I was an event scheduler for my boss at my last job. I lost it when I couldn't cope with losing my sister." While she told Marissa what she'd done before, Nancy picked up her fork and started eating. They were right, it was much easier now. "I'd love to work with you, but I have commitments at home that have to be dealt with."

"Oh, pish posh. We'll get that taken care of, won't we Lilac?" Lilac smiled and said that it would be a piece of cake. "Good. Now, you'll stay with me too. I'm alone in the house since my son has married. And the place has plenty of room. Oh, you'll need a car. I've never learned how to drive yet, so that'll be something we can work on as well."

Before she left with Marissa, she had her things moved to the house, her apartment being closed down, and an order for a new car. The limo that took them to the house was something that she'd never experienced before, and she enjoyed it. But as

171

soon as they pulled up in front of the *house*, she literally felt her jaw drop.

"This is not a house. You do know that, don't you?" Marissa just smiled. "This is…. This is…. I'm not sure what to say. But I can't stay here. This is just too much."

"This is the reason that I didn't tell you that you'd be living in a castle with me. It might well have overwhelmed you, and then where would I be?" They were handed out of the limo. Her luggage, the man told her, was already put in the blue room. "I didn't think that you'd want to be all girly. There is a yellow room as well as a pink one. You can move to any of them should you want. I'm just glad that you're here."

"Are you sure about this? For all you know, I'm this mass murderer." She realized what she'd said and asked her for forgiveness. "I just don't want you to find out something about me later and I'll be out on my ass again."

"Before you came here, you were thoroughly investigated. It isn't just you, dear. Anyone that comes in contact with this family has their lives looked into. We didn't connect you with your sister, as we're still trying to match up names to bodies that were found."

"James, he made it so you couldn't identify them. My sister had her teeth knocked out, and her face was…. It was beyond recognition. If it hadn't been for the tattoo that she had on her ankle, we wouldn't have known it was her." Marissa told her again how sorry she was. "You know, I thought that when I came here, I'd have who I thought was James arrested for his crimes — after I told him off and beat the shit out of him. I thought that it would give me closure, and I'd feel not so helpless again. But that didn't happen. I met his family."

"And you realized that there was hope again." Nancy nodded, tears flooding her eyes. "Come here, child. I want you to hug me. I need it."

They hugged for what seem like hours. It felt good. Nancy felt the last few months, all leading up to this point, just roll off her. She wasn't going to forget her sister or forgive the man who had murdered her in cold blood. But she knew that she was in a place that she could heal from both of them.

"Now, we're going to do that with each other whenever we're feeling down. But I have to tell you that since James has been taken care of, I feel as if I can move on with my life. There is much to tell you. Starting with, I'm a dragon." Nancy just stared at her, then laughed. "No, I'm a dragon. So are most of the people you've met today. Danburn? He's the king of us all. My son is his best friend, or one of them. Now, come along, let's have a look at that bedroom they put you in. My, it's going to be so nice to have you here. You have no idea. Oh, you'll need an office and—" Marissa had been heading up the stairs when she turned to her. "Aren't you coming, Nancy?"

"You're a dragon." Nodding, she smiled at her. "You're a dragon of a castle. And the king of dragons is Danburn. That nice man that goes all mushy when he talks about his wife and daughter. I suppose she's a dragon as well, the baby."

"Don't be silly. Of course, she is. Now, about that bedroom. You'll have your own maid to clean...."

As Marissa went up the stairs, still talking, Nancy shook her head and followed. If they were dragons, which she wasn't sure she believed, then.... Well, she didn't know what. But she had a place to stay and work, so she'd deal with it when one of them became a dragon.

She entered the most beautiful bedroom that she'd ever seen. "Do you like it? I can see that you do. I'm not even going to bother with the other rooms you can have. This one suits you. And from the window there, when we're flying, you'll be able to watch. Oh my, it's a sight to behold."

Nancy nodded. Yes, she was either in la-la land or she was now in the presence of greatness. Laughing to herself, she wondered what her last boss would have to say about that.

~*~

Griff pulled the last of the burned things from the castle basement. There was still plenty to do in Kip's home, but together, they were doing a great job of getting it cleaned up. As he put the debris in the ever growing pile, he decided that he needed a breather and set flames to the pile. Kip joined in a few minutes later.

"I had no idea that as a man you can do that." Griff said that he'd not either, that Lilac had asked him about it. "So, you tried it and it worked. That would save a lot of maneuverability when in a tight place, I'm thinking."

They both watched the fire burn. There was so much there that was wasted. Books had been destroyed. Chairs that were as old as Kip had been broken and left to rot in the home. Blankets that had been made by his grandmother had been infested with rats and other vermin. Even some of the things like trenchers, that had been used for plates that were centuries old, had been left with food in them and destroyed.

"I might have to steal some things from your museum. Right now, I don't have anything left but the walls to this." Kip laughed bitterly, his hurt and anger evident on his face. "They contacted me last night—my mother did, anyway. She and my father are living in France, and they wanted to know if, since I've cleaned up the mess here, I could send them some money. And she told me that they'd be arriving on the fourteenth of next month. She wondered if that was going to be enough time for me to get things set up for them to live here."

"Are you going to let them?" Kip shook his head. "When

174

are you going to tell them? I'm assuming that you've made arrangements to make it so they cannot enter."

"Yes, to that, but I told her last night. And told her that she'd not be able to enter due to me taking over. I don't think she believed me. Oh, and Kenneth, my older brother, he's been imprisoned. I don't know for what—don't care—but they could use some money to pay his bail too. That, I think she understood when I told her no fucking way." Kip sat on one of the stumps from the trees they'd had to have removed as well. The lawns looked better, but there had been a great deal of destruction there as well. "Do you suppose that my mate is out there, just waiting for me to find her and introduce her to my family?"

"Yes. I believe that. And we're your family, Kip. We always have been." Sitting on the other stump, he regarded his friend. "Have you told Danburn about what is going on here?"

"No, not yet. Having you know was hard enough on my pride." Kip looked at him as he continued. "All of us have envied Danburn and his relationship with his parents. I did more so, I think, because Fletcher, Danburn's father, was so kind to me. Whenever I was hurt by them, beaten until I could barely stand up, he would help me hide away for a few days. And I've never told anyone this, but Fletcher also paid for me to go to school when we were younger. He said it was the least he could do for what I had endured over the years."

Griff knew that Fletcher had done that for Kip, because Fletcher had asked him to keep an eye on Kip, to make sure that he had enough funds. He'd also told him to call him if his family came around, that he'd take care of it. They hadn't, so Griff often wondered what the man or dragon would have done to them had they bothered Kip while at school.

"I have money now. Not as much as the rest of you do, due to bailing my parents out of things all the time. But I'm finished with them. Much like you were with James. Kenneth and Bethany are grown, older than me by decades." Griff had wanted to know why his parents, or family for that matter, always needed money when they were dragons too. "Ah, that is a fantastic tale. When I was born, I was treated as if I wasn't worth the broken egg that I'd come from, according to my family. So one night, in desperation, I went to see Fletcher. He in turn took me before the council. I was only there to tell them that I couldn't live with them anymore. That they hurt me continually. But Fletcher had other reasons for taking me. After telling them what he'd found out about the family, he wished to take me with him to his home." Griff said that he remembered that. "Yes. I stayed with the Englishes just long enough to come into my own as a dragon. But you see, what I didn't know, but he did, was that my parents were abusing their tears."

"How does one abuse their tears?" Kip laughed; it was the first time he'd done that in a while, he'd bet. "This is going to be great, isn't it? Tell me."

"Okay. You know that we're not to use our tears for anything but what we deem we need. But my parents were using them to pay hitmen. People who'd been hired to burn down houses that they owned and had insurance on. All things, you're going to say, they could have done themselves. But they were lazy. And because Kenneth and Bethany were in on it as well, the council stripped them of their tears. I mean, they can cry, but they're just tears. Just like most humans cry."

"So, they've been unable to sustain themselves for centuries." Kip smiled and said that was right. "Holy shit, Kip. No wondered they're calling on you. Did they know that it was Fletcher that went after them?"

"Oh yes. They knew that I had been a large part of it as well. Lucky for me, I had someone that could take me in. My

176

family disowned me, just verbally, and they took care that I couldn't take my things from the castle. The broken stuff here, most of it was mine that you found in the sublevels. Where I lived for most of my younger years."

Griff hadn't known this — not all of it, anyway. No wonder Kip was so bitter about his family. They'd not just fucked him over, but themselves too. This was worse than the relationship that he'd had with James. Kip's entire family had turned on him, and had given him nothing in return for all his help with their troubles.

"You know when they're coming here?" He told him that they were to arrive on the fourteenth. Griff continued. "You come and stay with Lilac and I until this is ready. There isn't any sense in you still renting a home when we all have plenty of room."

"I was actually thinking about buying myself a home. It's not like I have good memories of this place. There isn't any kind of sentimental attraction to it either. I thought that I'd donate it to your museum. To put all the things that you've gathered for one." Griff was taken aback. That was quite a gift. "No, it's not. And if you use it for that, it'll make people happy to be in it. There hasn't been happiness in this place since I was born. You and Lilac take it — I'll buy me a nice house. I'm getting prepared for my mate when she gets here. It's only a matter of time, wouldn't you say?"

"Yes." Both of them got up; it was time to get to work, and he reached out to Lilac to tell her what Kip was planning to do. *He doesn't like the castle. And the only reason that I think he owns it is so that his family can't return.*

Will we have trouble with them? Before you answer that, let me tell you that'd I'd like to take them on. Kip is a wonderful person. Too nice for those people. Griff laughed and told her that she could

177

count on it. *Good. I'll see what it'll take to get it ready when it cools off enough. I want to help him out. You should see if he could not donate it to us, but rent it to us. That will piss his family off and give him some extra cash. Then later, he could have it back if he wants.*

He liked that idea and told her that. After telling her again how very much he loved her, he got back to work. The sooner they got this over with, the sooner Kip could find himself some peace. Well, the illusion of it at least. He'd never get that with his family out there somewhere.

Four hours later, the house and all the contents were cleaned out. After they'd taken the debris out, they had gone into each room and taken care of the larger things that had piled up. They could have done the burning inside the walls, but Kip hadn't wanted to heat it up any more than he had to. It was dangerous to the remaining trees surrounding the castle.

Deciding to meet with the others for dinner, they met up at the newest restaurant in town. It was a sub place, and they all could use some down time. After placing an order for Lilac and himself, he watched the people get overwhelmed by the size of the orders for those who had come to join them. Laughing to himself, he figured that they'd have to call ahead from now on. With six grown men and spouses, they had ordered thirty-five subs, all large, with drinks and chips.

It was an enjoyable evening, just friends and family. His mom joined them later with Nancy, and they all got to meet her. Griff thought that Kip was slightly disappointed that Nancy hadn't been his mate. But Griff knew that she was out there. Probably on her way here even as he thought about it.

If anyone needed to have someone love him, it would be Kip. He literally had no one that cared about him as much as these men did. His family were leaches, thieves, and liars. They'd blame everything on Kip that had befallen them, even if others had seen them commit the crime. He was the nicest person that he'd ever met, despite having the family that he did.

"I was thinking." He asked Lilac if he needed to bail her out when she did whatever it was. "Why do you think I'm going to get myself into trouble? Well, I usually do, but I can get myself out of it too."

Griff laughed. "What is it you've got planned?" She snuggled under his arm and he held her there. "Does this involve us making an early night of this? If so, I'm all game if you are."

"No. Why is every thought you have centered around sex?" He told her that he was a man. "Yes, you are at that. But what I was thinking was that we should have a fall fun festival for the town. It's been a good year so far. There are two new businesses here. Lots of people have jobs that didn't before. I think it would be good to have a fair, invite them all and do it up right."

"I like that idea. But you do know you have to run it by Danburn first?" She said that she knew that part. "And I'm betting that Elissa will want to help, as well as the others. Also, Rett. I'm sure that he'll approve it. Yeah, I love that idea. And the best part is, no bail money is involved."

"I hate you sometimes." Griff knew better and kissed her. "All right. You ask Danburn and I'll clear it with Rett. He's a great mayor, by the way. And Cassie is doing such a good job at the shelter too."

"I've heard that."

After standing up and kissing her again, Griff made his way to Danburn. If nothing else, he thought that he could use a project like this one to work on too.

Chapter 13

Dalton had nowhere to go, but she was told that she needed to use her built up vacation time or she'd lose it. The new company, the ones that had taken over the warehouse where she worked as a security guard, did not allow employees to turn vacation hours in for cash, nor let the time roll over to the next year. So, because of the new company allowing them to keep their built up time, Dalton now had nearly three months of mandatory vacation on her hands.

"And nothing to do." She had some money stashed away. Not a great deal, but if she wanted to go to the movies, she could also afford to get herself a drink *and* popcorn. "Like I go anywhere anymore."

Dalton couldn't remember the last time that she'd had free time on her hands. The apartment that she lived in was spotless, thanks to the first two days of her mandatory vacation. She didn't own a car, or any kind of transportation for that matter. Working so close to where she lived had made not owning that sort of thing great.

And since she wasn't home all that much, she didn't even

have a television to watch. Not that she'd do that either. Dalton had figured out yesterday morning that she was boring. Not only boring, but she was also a hermit.

"Not really."

Trying to nip talking to herself in the bud, she went to the kitchen to get a glass of tea. The apartment was warm—the air conditioner had gone out a few weeks ago. The landlord told her that she'd have to deal with the heat. Bastard.

Dalton was lucky in that she'd signed a lease on her apartment several years ago, and it stated that she was to have the same rate for as long as she lived there. Also, she didn't pay for cable or her trash pickup, nor did she have to fork over anything for repairs. But she had no idea who owned the building that she could complain to, so she did suffer the heat. Besides, it would be cooling off fairly soon, and she'd be freezing then.

Dalton looked at the door when someone knocked. She wasn't expecting anyone, hadn't ordered anything that was to be delivered. Though that stuff was supposed to be signed for by the man at the door. Dalton had never been sure why Carl was there. She was capable of opening and closing a door all by herself, but she figured that he was related to someone or he got free rent for doing the job. Whatever it was, she didn't go to the door for that very reason.

"Dalton Mueller? I'd like to speak to you." Sure, like that was going to have her opening a door for a stranger. She stood in the kitchen with the jug of tea in one hand, and slipped her gun out from her back, just in case. "My name is Wendell James. You might have heard of me."

Nope, her mind said. No one she knew even had James as a first name. When he pounded on the door again, really hitting the wood hard, she made her way to the door with her gun out and ready. Pulling the slide back, she knew that the man on the other side had to hear it. Pocketing the discharged ammo, she stood there waiting. Next move was his.

"I'm not going to hurt you. So, if you'd just open the door after putting the gun away, I'll talk to you." She said no. "Lady, this is just stupid. Open the fucking door before I have to knock it down."

"You do, and they'll be picking up your body." Pulling out her cell to call the police, she made sure that he could hear her side of the conversation. Never putting her gun down, she eyed the door carefully. "My name is Dalton Mueller. I have a man at my door that says that he's going to break it down to get in. His name is Wendell James. Or that's what he told me it was."

The man cursed — she heard that as plain as day. And when the door sounded like he'd shot it with a gun, Dalton did the only thing she could think of and fired at the broken wood. Falling back on her ass, she looked down at her chest and saw that he'd fired at her first, and she was bleeding. When the man looked at her from the hole that he'd put in the door, she fired until the magazine was empty. She'd seen him fall back, so knew that she'd at least hit him.

Picking up her phone with shaking hands, she heard the dispatcher screaming her name. Telling her that she'd had to kill the man because he'd shot her, Dalton wasn't sure she was going to make it.

"My chest is bleeding pretty badly. I can't see the man, but I'm sure that I hit him a couple of times." The dispatcher told her to remain calm, help was on its way. "Yeah, I'm not sure that's going to happen either. Christ, I hurt."

Before she passed out, which she thought was as good as done, Dalton put another clip in her gun before lying back.

Dalton felt someone touch her arm, and before she could lift her gun to fire again, her hand was grabbed. The man leaning over her didn't look familiar. When he smiled at her and told her that he was a police officer, she tried to pull her gun from him harder.

"I'm going to let your hand go, miss. And then I'm going to reach into my pocket and pull out my identification. All right?" She felt her hand being released and lifted the gun up to his forehead. "Christ, you're scary. My name is David Brooks. Here is my badge, as well as my ID. Please don't shoot me. My wife will be really pissed off at me if you do."

Looking at his badge, she couldn't focus on it. When he showed her his ID, she couldn't make it out either. But she was fading quickly and lowered her gun. It was draining what little strength she had.

"He tried to break in. Is he dead?" The man, Officer Brooks, said that he was. "It was self-defense. He left me no choice when he fired through my door."

"Yes, the dispatcher could hear it all. And it's been recorded. Did you know who it was?" Telling him that she didn't, he told her that the medics were here, but she had to relinquish her gun. "They can't work on you if they're afraid of you shooting them."

"You'll give it back?" He said that he would. "That man, he tried to break in. I didn't kill him until he fired first."

She blurred out for a little while, and found herself on a gurney and some people with her that she didn't know. Dalton asked one of them where she was. What they were doing.

"You're being life flighted to the hospital. Lady, you are one strong woman. You have three GSW to the chest—gunshot wounds—and you shouldn't be alive, much less talking. How about you rest up and we'll get you there to be fixed up."

She might have answered him but had no idea. The next

time she woke, there was a man in a mask standing over her. Dalton reached for her gun and realized that the officer had taken it. She asked the man who he was.

"I'm a surgeon that is going to try and remove the bullets. They told me that you were in and out of it, but I didn't believe them. We're going to give you something that will put you into a deeper sleep, Miss Mueller, so you let us — "

"Don't call my family. My brother and sister. I have an uncle. He's on my contact list." He asked her if she knew the number. "Yes. Just call my Uncle Eric. Don't call the others."

"I'll tell the officer. Now, you let this take you under and we'll see about getting these bullets out of you. All right?"

There was no chance to answer him. She felt the meds hit her system and she was out. All she could think about as she drifted away is that she didn't want her family to know.

~*~

Kip didn't care for this house. The first one he'd seen, three days ago, had been perfect. There wasn't any work to be done, except for minor things like a security system and a larger dining room, but the rest of it was just right. He looked at his realtor when the man's phone went off. Kip could tell right away that something bad had happened.

He wandered off to the kitchen again, to give the man privacy. He really didn't care for the layout of this room either. It was too stifling in here. Like even if you opened the windows, you'd still feel like you were in a cave.

Eric came into the room where he was and Kip grabbed him before he fell forward. "My niece. She's been shot." He asked him if she was all right. "They don't think she'll make it through the surgery. I told them that not only would she, but she'd be up and around soon too. They told me that one of the bullets had touched her heart, and they won't know how close

185

until they open her up. They made it sound like she was a can of soup that they'd be having for lunch."

"Where is she?" Eric told him that she lived in Columbus, that they'd life-flighted her to University Hospital. "Come on. I'll drive you there. I'm assuming they want you to come to them."

"Yes. And they said that she told them not to call her brother and sister. That's a good sign, isn't it, Kip? That she can tell them to not call them?" He said that he didn't know, but figured it might be. "I have to go. I'm sorry. Can we reschedule?"

"I'm taking you to the hospital, Eric. Come on, we'll leave the car here. And I'm buying the first house you showed me." Eric nodded and said that he'd put an offer in for him. Kip was trying his best to keep his mind off what had happened. "Come on now. I'll have you there as quickly as I can make it. You just sit tight."

They were both in the car when Eric pulled out his cell phone again. He asked Eric if he needed to have him pull over and he assured him that he was fine. He was calling Dalton's grandparents. Kip did pull over when the man started sobbing in the phone. When he shoved the phone in his direction, Kip took it only to hear someone crying at the other end.

"I'm sorry. I'm Kipling Newton. I'm taking Eric to the hospital now. He's very upset." The man told him he was as well, but he'd meet them there. "All right. I'll tell Eric."

"She's our son's child. Well, child doesn't cover it, as she's almost twenty-seven. I'm sorry, I'm babbling. Do you know anything more?" He said that he didn't. "We're leaving now. As soon as the cab gets here. We don't live far, so we'll be there before Eric. Tell him that, will you? Has anyone called Luann or Louis? Those are her deadbeat sister and brother. Damned fools, if you ask me."

"No sir. I guess just before they put her under, she told the surgeon not to call them, but to call her uncle." He laughed. "Eric seems to think that it would be like her to delay surgery to make sure things were right."

He'd not said that, but close enough. When the man cried again, Kip watched Eric. And when the man said that their cab had shown up, he closed the connection between them.

Eric was sick, throwing up in the bushes at the side of the road. Kip wondered what he might be getting himself into and had a sudden thought. She could be his mate. Leaning back on the seat, he tried to wrap his mind around that.

He kept telling himself that it was highly unlikely that she was, but his mind was telling him to be prepared. She already sounded like someone that he'd get. Hard headed, he'd bet. She carried a gun, so there was that.

When Eric got back in the car, Kip handed him a pack of gum. They didn't speak the rest of the way in. Eric did receive and make several phone calls. None of them pertained to him, so he really didn't pay attention to them. Traffic was brutal, for which he was glad. It gave him less time to think about a possibility of a mate. When they pulled into the parking lot, Eric jumped out before him and Kip made his way slowly to the right floor.

"Hello, Mr. Newton. I'm Charley Mueller, and this is my wife Fern. We're Dalton's paternal grandparents. Though we did raise her from the age of twelve. Nasty business that." Kip told him that he was sorry about all this. That he could go on home. "I'd rather you stayed, if you don't mind. Eric is going to need a friend if she doesn't make it."

He didn't tell him that he'd only just met the man four days ago. Nor did he mention that he was looking for a house through him. None of it came up, so he sat with the family to wait with them.

Fern came to sit by him. "You're probably thinking that you tried to do a good man a favor and got caught up in drama. There is a great deal of it with her sister and brother. Theirs, not hers. Dalton was as much a black sheep to them as anyone would be that was as brilliant as she is. And she's not one to suffer fools easily. Her parents, and her two siblings, didn't give her enough when she was a little guy. So, she's shut most people out of her life." Kip told her that he was having issues like that himself. "Then you understand. Dalton graduated from high school when she was twelve. It might have been sooner, but her parents had been killed and it set her back a little bit. Not emotionally, but dealing with Louis and Luann. They're not nice children either."

"What happened, do you know?" She told him what she knew. An officer who was first on the scene to find her had told her all that he could. "Dalton, does she normally carry a gun? I mean, she was lucky to have been armed, but I was just wondering."

"She used to be a police officer in another state. Came back here to live about five years ago. Dalton is a good girl, but she had it rough growing up, and it made her somewhat leery of people." Fern laughed. "That's certainly an understatement. She doesn't trust many people."

"I don't either except the friends that I have. They're all I have left." Kip thought it was nice to be able to talk to someone. A person that wasn't around his woes all the time. And Fern was a good listener too. "I should warn you, I'm not human. If you'd rather I wasn't here, then I can go because of that."

"No. I don't care what you are so long as you don't hurt us. What are you, anyway?" Kip told her he was a dragon. "My goodness. I didn't know that they were still around. Or for that matter that there even was any."

"Yes, there are a few of us left. Mostly we keep to ourselves as well." She nodded, and they both watched a man wearing scrubs walk by them. He met up with the family in the next waiting room. "Dalton's in good hands here. This is the best hospital you could be at for things like this."

"She's all we have. Eric is her uncle. Dalton's mother was his sister." Kip nodded, not really sure why he'd need to know that, but she was stressed out. "I'm blabbing again. I'm sorry."

"That's all right. Really it is. Eric was showing me houses when he got the call. I didn't think that he was fit to drive, so I brought him." She nodded and asked him if he'd found a house. "I did, as a matter of fact. It's big and set off the road. It's too big for one person, but I'm expecting a mate to come around someday, and we can fill it, I suppose."

He hadn't meant to say it that way, but she patted him on the cheek and he didn't feel quite so embarrassed. When another man in scrubs walked by them again, he talked to both Charley and Eric when Fern went to get her a soda.

"Mr. and Mrs. Mueller?" Charley stood up and so did he and Eric. Fern was just getting off the elevator when the man started to tell them who he was. Charley held onto his wife's hand and said that he was ready. "Dalton is in grave condition. The bullet that touched her heart did a little more damage than we'd hoped. But she's young and fit, so she has a better chance than most. We removed three bullets from her chest and another in her arm. But for now, we're only concentrating on the one that did the most damage."

"How long before she's out of the woods, Doc? I mean, I know you said grave, and I'm an old enough man to know what that means. But you do have some kind of goal for her, don't you?" Charley wiped at his tears as he continued. "She's a fighter, my Dalton."

"She is at that. And to answer your question, sir, all I can tell you is that every hour that she lives, that only makes her stronger. Dalton lost a great deal of blood, which we're working to get to her."

He looked at Kip and asked if he could speak to him alone. When he stepped away from the family, he knew that the doctor was a tiger, and that he also knew what Kip was. Kip already knew what he was going to ask of him.

"I'm mated to a wonderful woman. And if I were to help this young woman along by giving her my blood, no matter the circumstances, I'd be needing my own transfusion when she was finished with me. Are you mated?" Kip told him that he wasn't, but if he was going to ask him to help her along, they had to tell her family. "I can do that. I'm assuming that since you're here with them, they know that you're not human."

"The grandmother does. I'm sure that she's told her husband. Her uncle knows as well." He nodded and asked if he could talk to them with him. "I can do that. Easily. I'm very old and extremely powerful, Doc, so you should be prepared to tell them what that will mean as well."

"Thank you. You might be the difference she needs to pull through this."

They both sat with the three of them. Eric was all for it, saying that he wanted her to live no matter how it happened. But the grandparents had questions.

"What if your mate comes along, young man? What will happen between the two of you?" He started to answer Charley when he had another question. "Just how powerful are you? I mean, with age, I'm to understand comes more. Unlike me, who just loses it every year."

It had been a joke—it failed, but he didn't seem to mind.

Kip thought about how to answer him when he just put out his hand and blew fire onto it. The flame burned for some time before he put his hands together to put it out.

"I'm very old. Well before people were plentiful around here. I'm a dragon of good standing. And if my mate does come along, and it's not Dalton, she won't be upset because this happened before her." Fern asked if Dalton was his mate. "I don't know. I've never met her before. But I can tell you that if you agree for me to help her along, my blood will heal her a hundred times faster and better than if she doesn't have it."

They gave him permission and he was suited up in scrubs. They didn't want him to bring in germs because this might not work—they weren't taking any chances.

As soon as he entered the room where she was, all he could smell was death. It was all over the young woman like a blanket. Walking to the bed, he saw several machines around her, blood dripping into her IV, as well as a tube down her throat. That was going to be removed first.

As soon as it was free of her lungs, he stood over the bed and leaned to her throat. She was his. This woman was his mate.

Opening a vein to give her the most of himself via the fastest route, Kip thought of what Dalton was going to say to him when she woke. Giving her more than the few drops that the doctor had asked for, he had to laugh to himself. His mate was going to pissed, he knew it. And Kip was actually looking forward to her taming him.

Before You Go...

HELP AN AUTHOR
write a review
THANK YOU!

Share your voice and help guide other readers to these wonderful books. Even if it's only a line or two your reviews help readers discover the author's books so they can continue creating stories that you'll love. Login to your favorite retailer and leave a review. Thank you.

AWARD WINNING, BESTSELLING AUTHOR

Kathi Barton, winner of the Pinnacle Book Achievement award as well as a best-selling author on Amazon and All Romance books, lives in Nashport, Ohio with her husband Paul. When not creating new worlds and romance, Kathi and her husband enjoy camping and going to auctions. She can also be seen at county fairs with her husband who is an artist and potter.

Her muse, a cross between Jimmy Stewart and Hugh Jackman, brings her stories to life for her readers in a way that has them coming back time and again for more. Her favorite genre is paranormal romance with a great deal of spice. You can visit Kathi online and drop her an email if you'd like. She loves hearing from her fans. aaronskiss@gmail.com.

Follow Kathi on her blog: http://kathisbartonauthor.blogspot.com/

www.ingramcontent.com/pod-product-compliance
Lightning Source LLC
Chambersburg PA
CBHW032138170626
46808CB00006B/2285